A SWEEPING ASSAULT

The Black Eagles had faced eight East Germans on the right flank. With five of them now down, the survivors made an instinctive withdrawal.

Falconi knew it was time to change directions and slam into the other group of unsuspecting strangers. Again he gave his commands in the simplest terms as he spoke into the small radio.

"Reverse! Reverse!"

Horny Galchaser, who had just fired a grenade from his launcher, stopped in midstride. He broke his weapon open for reloading.

The bullet that hit him was a wild one. It had been fired only for effect by an East German out of sight in the thick brush.

Everyone else was too busy reversing the direction of the attack in order to swing back and hit the unsuspecting enemy who had counted on finding them much sooner. Thrown off balance, the Reds had stopped. The coordinated assault of the Black Eagles hit them hard. Volleys of M16 bullets swept through them, downing four before the remaining five broke and fled. . . .

THE BLACK EAGLES
by Jon Lansing

#1: HANOI HELLGROUND (1249, $2.95)
They're the best jungle fighters the United States has to offer, and no matter where Charlie is hiding, they'll find him. They're the greatest unsung heroes of the dirtiest, most challenging war of all time. They're THE BLACK EAGLES.

#2: MEKONG MASSACRE (1294, $2.50)
Falconi and his Black Eagle combat team are about to stake a claim on Colonel Nguyen Chi Roi—and give the Commie his due. But American intelligence wants the colonel alive, making this the Black Eagles' toughest assignment ever!

#3: NIGHTMARE IN LAOS (1341, $2.50)
There's a hot rumor that the Russians are secretly building a nuclear reactor in Laos. And the Black Eagles are going to have to move fast—to prevent the nuclear fallout from hitting the fan!

#4
PUNGI PATROL

THE BLACK EAGLES

BY JOHN LANSING

ZEBRA BOOKS
KENSINGTON PUBLISHING CORP.

ZEBRA BOOKS

are published by

Kensington Publishing Corp.
475 Park Avenue South
New York, N.Y. 10016

First printing: June, 1984

Printed in the United States of America

Dedicated to
the French soldiers and legionnaires
who fought in Indochina, 1946–1954.
Although always short on personnel and equipment,
they were never lacking in courage and determination.

Special acknowledgment to Patrick Andrews and
W. L. Fieldhouse

PROLOGUE

The Old Man squatted on his haunches in the village square and stared mournfully down at the dust.

He had known war for over twenty years now. First the Japanese had come to form what they termed their Sphere of Co-prosperity with the peoples of Asia. The Old Man and his fellow villagers had endured the Nipponese Empire's brand of administration and government until the end of World War II. Then the Sons of Heaven had been driven back to their home islands to recover under the benevolent occupation and tutelage of their conquerors. As soon as they had been picked up and dusted off by the Americans, they began to enrich themselves manufacturing automobiles and electronic gadgetry based on transistor technology.

But the situation wasn't so pleasant in Indochina. The immediate postwar period was marked by the emergence of a new brand of tormentor who appeared in the guise of national liberators. This fresh batch of troublemakers called themselves the Viet Minh and proclaimed to people like the Old Man and the inhabitants of the little hamlet, that they had come to deliver them from the clutches of the French oppressors. These strange nationalists, who practiced and preached a political philosophy as foreign as that of France, brought the war into the very huts of the village. They forced the people to hide arms, food, other supplies for them. At the same time they took many young men away for intense indoctrination and training so that these youths would have the privilege of fighting and dying in this new war of independence.

Naturally, when the French soldiers came around in their campaign against the Viet Minh, they would sometimes find the things hidden under the huts of the villagers. This would mean quick and severe punishment despite the most vocal and sincere protestations of innocence or good intent. In a space of only three years, this small farming community had been burned down not less than seven times.

Yet these unfortunate people asked of all the combatants only to be left alone and allowed to grow enough rice to survive. "Why not take the struggle into the city where there are many more people?" they begged.

"Because *you* are the true revolution!" the Viet Minh had answered.

And the French had to fight there because that was the place where the Communist guerrillas preferred to make their war. Thus, the Old Man and his people found themselves stuffed down a meat grinder—and it was their blood and their flesh coming out the other end.

Now the Old Man glanced up at these new soldiers who had recently arrived in the settlement. They spoke a language he did not understand, and these strangers made their wants and demands known with inarticulate

8

grunts and shouts which were emphasized with kicks and punches.

The young women had already been raped. They had been herded into one of the larger huts and the soldiers had enjoyed them for a couple of hours before tiring of the sport. These women, shamefaced and disgraced, had rearranged their clothing as best they could for modesty's sake. This was difficult because the soldiers, impatient in their lust, had ripped the apparel from their bodies. The ravished women, bruised and in some instances beaten, lowered their eyes and returned to their homes. Each had endured physical assaults by at least three of the foreign soldiery.

The Old Man had a deep secret. He could not only read and write his own language, but in French as well. He had found it to his advantage to conceal this from all the warring factions involved in this enigmatic struggle, and none of the villagers had betrayed him. His knowledge of the colonial power's language now helped him to recognize who these new soldiers were. Each sported a cloth strip sewn over the breast pocket of his uniform. One of these was obviously the man's name, but the other, proudly mounted on the left side of the jackets, was black with gold letters that spelled out: U.S. Army.

The Old Man knew they were Americans and that, in this year of 1964, their presence was growing in Vietnam.

The senior officer wore cloth insignia sewn to his collar. Now that the enjoyment of the women was over, he barked a few terse orders and his soldiers herded all the younger males into a group at the far end of the cluster of huts. The Old Man, looking ancient and frail, had been left with the women and children.

The village men were driven with rifle butts into a tight group as other soldiers, their weapons ready, formed up in a semicircle around them. More orders were barked and the invaders aimed their rifles at the packed mass of rice farmers. Some, realizing what was going to happen, held out their hands in imploring gestures for mercy.

But suddenly there was the rapid and loud staccato fire of rifles belching flame and bullets.

Slugs slammed into the hapless prisoners, the force of their impact throwing the men into each other as the steel-jacketed rounds tore into their bodies dumping them to the ground like bloody bundles of rags.

A few, who had either been missed or only slightly wounded, made a break for the safety of the nearby jungle. They only got a few meters before a fresh fusillade slammed into their backs, spinning them around to fall face-up between two outlying huts.

It seemed strangely quiet after the firing had stopped.

One of the soldiers, wearing chevrons on his arm, looked from the carnage to the officer. He snapped to attention and saluted. *"Ist das alles, Kamerad Hauptmann?"*

The officer nodded. *"Ja. Nun Ich möchte Feldlager gehen."*

CHAPTER ONE

The promotion had come as a surprise, but not a particularly pleasant one.

Not that Robert Falconi didn't like the idea of being a major. Being appointed up to field-grade rank was something he wanted, but not under these particular circumstances. None of the enlisted men in the Black Eagles had been upped in rank, and they were stuck out in the boondocks at the unit's base camp while he was here in Saigon waiting to see Chuck Fagin, the Central Intelligence Agency's case officer assigned to the elite outfit Falconi commanded.

The Black Eagles was a special detachment made up of the best jungle fighters in Southeast Asia. There were representatives from the United States Army, Navy, and Marine Corps on the roster along with a South Vietnamese officer, an Australian Special Air Service staff sergeant and a master sergeant from the Republic of Korea's crack marines.

Each of these men, no matter what his particular

branch of service or nationality, was an expert *par excellence* in his own special brand of mayhem or military skills. They were familiar with weapons of all nations—particularly those from behind the Iron Curtain—and could handle implements for killing that ranged from electronically controlled antitank weaponry down to the crossbows and knives that best met the need for silent killing in gut-level fighting.

And, of course, when explosives were required on a mission, the Black Eagles could produce the right boys for that noisy type of destruction too.

The more sophisticated skills such as communications, land navigation, foreign languages, combat intelligence, military operations, small-unit tactics, and other exotic soldiering tools were also within the realm of knowledge of the Black Eagles.

They were the enforcement arm of SOG—Special Operations Group—and drew the most sensitive and dangerous war missions , those that had to be conducted deep inside enemy territory. They had penetrated North Vietnam on two occasions, and their last mission had been behind Pathet Lao lines in Laos where they had blown up an ill-conceived nuclear power plant the Soviets had wanted to construct there.

But now, while tightly locked into this most perilous type of warmaking, they faced an even more insidious enemy. The CIA man, Chuck Fagin, was sure that Communist espionage and intelligence agents were closely monitoring their activities despite all efforts to thwart such compromises. Thus, the Black Eagles had been confined to their sparse quarters out in an army Special Forces B-Team operational area while things were sorted out. They had been on two dangerous missions without as much as five minutes R&R—Rest and Recreation—and no one, not even these superbly trained and conditioned veterans could maintain such a restrictive and nerve-racking existence for long without cracking up.

The only question now was what was the limit of their endurance.

Their commander, Major Robert Mikhailovich Falconi, had been billeted at SOG headquarters at Peterson Air Force Base for the precise purpose of getting the briefing on their next mission.

Chuck Fagin opened his office door and stepped in. He nodded to the young woman seated at the desk. "How are you this morning, Andrea?"

"Fine, thank you, Chuck," she replied. The young woman, an attractive Eurasian, wore the uniform of the ARVN—Army of the Republic of South Viet Nam.

Fagin noted her military apparel. "I see there's been a change here."

Andrea smiled slightly and reached up to tap one of the new epaulettes mounted on her shirt's shoulders. "Yes. The administrative people finally caught up to me. The rank of major had been temporary for Operation Hanoi Hellground. They put me back at my permanent grade of second lieutenant."

"And that included a reduction in salary too, I presume," Fagin remarked.

"I'm afraid so. But at least Falcon has been promoted," Andrea said.

"Then he should be happy about that."

"He's upset because none of his men have been recognized for their service in the Black Eagles," Andrea said.

13

Fagin sighed. "His promotion was routine and due to take place as per the ARs. He had the necessary time in grade and service along with the other qualifications. So it was simply a matter of administrative policy to promote him. In fact, the orders came from the Pentagon, not a local commander. But I've purposely kept the enlisted men on a low profile until I check out that request for their roster."

"It came through Colonel Ngai Quang," Andrea reminded him. "He's one of the most trusted officers in ARVN's intelligence branch."

"Maybe," Fagin said. "But—"

"Evidently that's not good enough for you," Andrea said.

"Clayton Andrews and Falconi built up the Black Eagles to be as clandestine as possible," Fagin remarked. "I intended to follow that custom, but that fell through after I was ordered to turn over their entire roster to Ngai—and given no reason for it other than we're supposed to cooperate with the South Vietnamese as much as possible."

"Maybe you're just naturally a nervous and suspicious person," Andrea suggested.

Fagin nodded his agreement. "You bet! And between my nerves and my untrusting nature, I've managed to keep myself alive and well in this twilight world of intelligence and dirty tricks, my dear." He walked to the door of his inner office. "I presume that Falconi is on the premises."

"Yes," Andrea answered. "Shall I send for him?"

"Please," Fagin answered. "But I must admit I'm not looking forward to meeting with him."

Andrea smiled at the CIA man. "I can't blame

14

you for that." She turned to her phone. "I'll have him sent up from the billets."

Second Lieutenant Andrea Thuy, of French and Vietnamese parentage, was a beautiful young woman. Five feet, six inches tall, she was lean and trim yet had large breasts and rounded hips that accented her femininity despite the military clothing she generally wore.

She had been born in a village west of Hanoi, where she'd enjoyed a happy girlhood until the coming of the Communist Viet Minh. Their visit had definitely not been one of pacification or even one to win the hearts and minds of the people in the region. The Communists had come to punish the villagers and to make such an example of them that none of the peasants in the locality would ever dare to do what Andrea's hamlet had done — defy them by ignoring their demands for support.

Although she had been only three years old at the time, she could remember with vivid horror and revulsion the rapine and slaughter visited upon these innocent people. Her own parents had been shot down in the wanton massacre that left but one survivor — Andrea Roget, infant daughter of Doctor Gaston Roget, a French missionary physician who had lived for years among the indigenous population of rural Indochina.

French soldiers arrived several hours after the carnage. They explored the burned village, examining the cadavers sprawled between the huts until they stumbled across the lone survivor of the massacre — Andrea. One grizzled paratrooper picked the little girl up in his brawny arms and cooed to her, "Oh, *pauvre enfant,* we will take you away from all this *horreur.*"

Andrea had ended up in a Catholic orphanage in Hanoi. Here, since all records in the village had been destroyed, no one knew exactly who the little girl was. She could say her first name, but never quite mastered the last. The nuns decided to call her Thuy, and Andrea Roget became Andrea Thuy.

The years at the orphanage had been happy ones. Andrea grew straight and beautiful, getting not only a good education, but learning responsibility as more and more parentless children came in from the war-devastated countryside to live at the orphanage. Andrea did her part to take care of them. And, because she was such a brilliant student, she helped teach school to the waifs who had come under the tender care of the *Les Soeurs de la Charité* — the Sisters of Charity.

But, once again, the war ruined her life. The Communist victory at Dien Bien Phu brought about the closing of the orphanage in Hanoi. The nuns and their small charges fled south, finally settling into a small mission near Attopeu, Laos.

Despite the more rustic and primitive setting, Andrea continued to prosper physically and spiritually under the kindness of the nuns.

Then the Pathet Lao came.

These particular Communist zealots were the most fanatic and murderous of the various followers of Marxism. They were even more terrible than the Viet Minh.

Andrea was fifteen at the time, thus she was included in the game of rape. The nuns and all the older girls were brutally ravished, then the mission was burned to the ground. The unfortunate *Soeurs de la Charité*, because they were French, were executed. The nuns, naked and shamed, were dragged to the burning buildings and flung, alive and screaming, into the flames. The Oriental eyes passed on to her by her mother, saved

Andrea's life. The raiders thought she was just another native girl.

After the Pathet Lao had abandoned their fun, Andrea's instincts told her to move south away from the Red horror that had descended on her life. She gathered up the smaller children and began a journey to some obscure safety she could only hope existed.

After two weeks of slow, tortuous travel, Andrea came upon a patrol of ARVN troops. Her first reaction, upon sighting the soldiers, was one of instinctive fear and alarm. When it became apparent there would be no repetition of the mistreatment she had already endured, Andrea relaxed and breathed a quick prayer of thanks under her breath.

The commander of the detachment, a young lieutenant, followed the Standard Operating Procedure for such situations and had the children sent on to higher headquarters for interrogation and eventual placement into some sanctuary.

During Andrea's interview with South Vietnamese intelligence officers, they learned that she not only was well acquainted with areas now held by various enemy factions, but was fluent in three languages—Vietnamese, French, and Laotian. They became so interested in the girl and her potential as an agent for them that they instigated a thorough background investigation of her past life. It was through this painstaking background check that she learned she was the daughter of Monsieur le Docteur Gaston Roget.

Andrea was taken to a colonel for further questioning. He was a pleasant, round-faced man who smiled readily and spoke to her in a friendly manner. After some rather enjoyable preliminary conversation, he got to the point. "Tell me, Andrea," he said. "What do you think of the Pathet Lao and the Viet Minh?"

A hidden side of Andrea was revealed at that moment. She pointed to the pistol on the man's hip. "If you give me that gun, *monsieur,* I will kill every one of those devils!" Andrea exclaimed.

"Would you be willing to fight them in another manner?" the colonel asked.

Andrea, still angry, nodded. "Of course, *monsieur!*"

"You are well versed in languages," he said. "And seem to display a natural talent to learn them. Would you like to learn more? Tai, Japanese, and even English?"

"Would this help me to kill Communists?" Andrea asked.

The colonel decided to speak to her as a mature young woman rather than a lost girl. *"Mais oui, mademoiselle."*

"But how?"

"By becoming an agent and going into their midst in various disguises to do mischief against them," the officer explained. "But in order to do such work, you must receive specialized training. And I guarantee, it will be a most vigorous and thorough education."

"Then let us begin, *monsieur,*" Andrea told him.

In order to confuse any potential tracers of her true identity, Andrea never reclaimed her legal father's name of Roget. Instead, because all church and religious school records listed her only as Andrea Thuy, she kept that same identification.

The young woman spent two years in specialized training. She learned more languages and the special skills required for her dangerous line of work. Various killing methods, including the use of poisons and drugs, were added to her repertoire. Andrea also was given a thorough course in the identities and faces of various Communist leaders and bigwigs in the north.

Then they turned her loose on those people she hated with such a passion.

In a twenty-four-month period, Andrea killed no less than four top leaders of the Communists during various missions to the north. Her hatred and her desire to destroy these individuals were so strong that she was even willing to use her body in order to gain their confidence before administering the deadly *coup de grâce* and ending their efforts toward promoting world socialism once and for all.

Her operations finally brought her to the attention of SOG, especially to Clayton Andrews, the CIA case officer charged with creating an elite killer/raider unit. This dedicated American intelligence agent was extremely impressed with the beautiful young woman. He pulled a few strings and saw to it that Andrea was sent to Langley Air Force Base in Virginia to the special CIA school. There her already highly rated death-dealing skills were increased to an even higher degree.

Her return to Southeast Asia was marked with an assignment to SOG's Black Eagle detachment led by an energetic young captain named Robert Falconi.
Andrea Thuy was now commissioned in the South Vietnamese army as a second lieutenant and given a temporary appointment as major.

The Black Eagles' first assignment, named Operation Hanoi Hellground, consisted of a direct action mission against a Communist pleasure palace where various Red bigwigs met to enjoy sinful pleasures denied to the general population under their cruel leadership. It had been a knockdown, drag-out series of fire fights and hand-to-hand fighting, and Major Andrea Thuy had performed faultlessly throughout the entire operation. All involved had agreed she had been superb.

Andrea's downfall had nothing to do with her fighting ability; it was her womanhood that brought about the reduction in both her responsibility and rank. She fell in love with Captain Robert Falconi.

When Chuck Fagin took over Clayton Andrews's job and found his primary combat leader and top intelligence operative involved in a red-hot romance, he had no choice but to pull one of them out of active ops. Such an emotional entanglement would not only endanger their own lives through muddled or passionate judgments, but also those of the other Black Eagles — and their missions.

Falconi, his battle career even more diversified and wider than Andrea's, was the natural choice to continue on the Black Eagles' missions.

The young woman's role was changed from that of an operative to administrative director. Andrea accepted the decision as only being proper, but deep in her heart there still burned the unquenchable hatred for the Viet Cong, the Pathet Lao, and the North Vietnamese, and she patiently awaited her chance to jump back into the fray once more.

CHAPTER TWO

Major Robert M. Falconi strode beside his MP escort down the hall toward the isolated office of Chuck Fagin.

They paused at the door and the soldier rapped on it. There was the buzzing sound of an electronic latch and the portal snapped open. "Major Falconi, ma'am," the MP announced to Andrea Thuy.

Falconi walked past him and waited for his escort to withdraw. As soon as the door shut, Andrea rushed to his arms. She held up her face to be kissed. After this affectionate greeting, her mood became grimmer. "How long must we wait?" she asked in a voice near pouting. "We've not slept together since your return."

Falconi had known she would launch into complaining about his avoidance of her since he'd flown in from the base camp. "As soon as my guys get some pussy, I'll get some," he said.

"Not a very elegant way of putting it," Andrea said coldly. "That makes me feel like some cheap bar girl."

"Don't be ridiculous," Falconi said testily.

"Well, what kind of women do you think that bunch

would be rutting on?" Andrea asked. "We're lovers, Robert, *lovers!* That's supposed to make a difference."

"The detachment is rotting out there in that fucking bunker," Falconi said. "The only recreation they've got is drinking beer and telling old war stories while they stare at four walls of sandbags. Since returning to Saigon, I've purposely stayed in my quarters with only a fifth of scotch to keep me company. There's no way in hell I'm going to cut loose while the guys are still locked up like that."

"You're not being fair to us," Andrea said. Then she gave up the argument and sighed. "Chuck said for you to go right in when you arrived."

"Thanks." He walked to the door leading to the inner office, then stopped and turned to face her. "You understand, don't you, Andrea?"

"All I know is that you're putting me on the level of a street whore," she replied.

"I'm sorry you feel that way," Falconi said. He knocked on the door.

"Yeah?" Fagin's voice, from inside his office, was gruff and muffled.

Falconi entered the small room and went directly to the chair in front of the desk. He plopped down onto it without ceremony. "I've been told there's a mission going down for the Black Eagles."

"Right. We've received numerous reports — and complaints — that American troops have been committing atrocities against local people out in the field," Fagin answered, also not wanting to waste time. "These war crimes range from rape to wholesale slaughter, not to mention burning entire villages down to the nubs."

"What outfits?" Falconi asked, concerned. "That sure

as hell isn't going to help our cause here."

"As far as we know they're not our guys," Fagin answered. "All investigations of the incidents show that there were not American troops anywhere near the areas where the atrocities took place."

"Then somebody in American uniforms is committing war crimes," Falconi mused. "They must be Caucasians to pull it off convincingly."

"From all descriptions, yes," Fagin responded. "But we don't know who. There's been a lot of theories. Maybe Russians or ex-Foreign Legionnaires from the old war that defected to the Reds. Whoever the bastards are, they're playing hell with attitudes towards us."

"How bad is the situation?"

"Bad enough that there's a deep rift growing between us and the South Vietnamese," Fagin said. *"We* know for sure they're not our guys, but it's happening so much that our allies are becoming suspicious—not that I blame them any."

"What can be done about it"

"That's where the Black Eagles come in," Fagin said "This stuff's going down along the coast in the vicinity north of Danang and west of Highway 1."

"Pretty rugged country up there," Falconi said.

"Sure is," Fagin agreed. "The big problem is the proximity of Danang and Hué. Those are areas heavily infiltrated with Red agents. It's been impossible to ferret out the sons-of-bitches. They can be anyone from employees in military laundries to high-ranking officials. We have no secrets in the area."

"Mmmm," Falconi mused. "And what'll happen when we show up?"

"The Reds will probably know you're coming before

the local commanders," Fagin said. "I'm still pissed off about having to hand over that roster to Colonel Ngai."

"Ngai's been around a long time," Falconi snapped. "I think you're turning into a Nervous Nellie."

"I like being a Nervous Nellie," Fagin remarked calmly. "I never said I wanted to be the *best* CIA case officer, only the *oldest*. And I'll attain that goal by being careful."

"And by keeping some guys strapped down out in the boonies," Falconi said. "They're not going to be able to take much more confinement without a break, Fagin. You'd better relax a bit before too much more time goes by."

"I'll decide after this mission," Fagin said.

"How soon do we go on it?"

"P.D.Q.," Fagin answered. "Because of the security nightmare I've mentioned, we'll be putting you ashore from a sub. If you show up on any military installation within close proximity of the Operational Area, your presence will be immediately broadcast to enemy units. So you'll be taken to a spot off the coast and go in on rubber boats. Stash the rafts then head for the interior. Your exfiltration will be planned later."

"And in the meantime we're supposed to wander all over that part of the country until we find out who's doing all the bad stuff in our name, right?"

"Right," Fagin answered. "And eliminate or capture the bastards. The latter action is of number one priority. The CIA wants some prisoners so we can wring 'em dry." He slipped a packet of papers across the desk to Falconi. "There're the op plans. Have your boys work them into an operations order and have at it."

Falconi wordlessly took the papers.

"By the way," Fagin continued, "how's your team sergeant working out? I remember you were slightly worried about him before the last mission."

"Gordon wised up," Falconi said. "The guys are calling him Top now. I figured they would never accept him, but he finally realized he wasn't in a conventional unit anymore. He's as relaxed and easygoing as they are when it comes to the ARs, and he's a damn good man under fire."

"Great!" Fagin said. "I was really worried about him. Thought I might have to pull him out."

"Like you did Andrea?"

"You shouldn't have fucked her," Fagin said bluntly.

"There's more to it than that," Falconi said.

"That makes it worse," Fagin said. "If she wasn't such a topnotch intelligence analyzer I'd have canned her a long time ago rather than use her as an analyst and administrator."

"I won't argue with you about it."

"Wouldn't do you any good."

"But I will pick a fight over my boys being stuck in isolation and sent on missions without a break," Falconi said coldly.

"I'll see what I can do," Fagin said.

"They're coming back after this mission, and I'm not taking any shit from you about it," Falconi warned him. "They haven't had a piece of ass or even enjoyed a drink in a bar for three months now."

Fagin's face reddened with anger. "Don't lecture at me, goddamn it! This job is tough enough without you giving me a ration of crap. Do you think I like holding those guys under wraps like that? I'm doing it until I figure out if it's safe for them to return to Saigon. If the bad guys can finger your people, they'll be out to either hit or snatch 'em. And I won't chance that. The missions of the Black Eagles are too damned important to take even the slightest risk."

Falconi stood up and shoved the operations plans under one brawny arm. "Remember what I told you, Fagin."

Then he turned and walked abruptly from the office.

The rest of the Black Eagles remained in a state of unsettled apprehension as they stayed in the base camp and waited for the return of their commanding officer.

They were a diversified group, yet somehow the dissimilarity of their backgrounds was the galvanizing element that made the detachment the smooth running team that it was.

The second-in-command was a Vietnamese first lieutenant named Nguyen Van Dow. A diminutive five feet, three inches tall, and weighing in at only a hundred and twenty pounds, he was well acquainted with the Viet Cong enemy due to having once been one. His disillusionment and eventual defection to the south came primarily as the result of his fiancée's being forced into becoming a "joy girl"—the official term for camp prostitutes in the Viet Cong. Nguyen's attempt to rectify the situation and see the commissar responsible punished, opened his eyes to the corruption and double standard in the "classless" society of Communism. When he found the girl he loved had been driven to suicide, Nguyen Van Dow killed the Red official who had degraded her, then headed south with his weapons, plenty of intelligence, and a burning desire to kill all the Viet Cong. He joined the ARVN and fought with distinction against his former comrades. His combat record was such that he earned a place in the Black Eagles when it was activated under SOG's guiding hand. By then he was lieutenant, and his new friends in the freshly formed detachment soon dubbed him "Dinky Dow" — Vietnamese for "Crazy" — due to his fanatical fighting spirit and ability. And, if Dinky Dow had any weaknesses, it was this uncontrollable battle fever that sometimes interfered with his combat leadership capabilities.

Master Sergeant Duncan Gordon was the detachment sergeant. Called "Top" by the men, he was the senior noncommissioned officer in the Black Eagles. Not only responsible for forming plans and operations, he maintained the necessary discipline to keep the unit on an even keel. Heavyset and balding, Gordon was a dark-haired man, who at thirty-five years of age had over seventeen years in the army. A thoroughly dedicated professional soldier, his devotion to military life had cost him his marriage. It was this zeal that had at first made him unpopular when he arrived in the detachment. He had taken the place of a well-liked team sergeant who had been killed in action. This sergeant, called "Top" by the men, had enjoyed a special place in their affections. Even under the best of conditions Gordon would have experienced resentment from the troops. But this difficult situation was made worse when Gordon started out on the wrong foot with the men. His method of doing things strictly by the book and his unbending adherence to Army regulations brought him into early conflict with the individualistic members of the Black Eagles.

But eventually, his bravery and efficiency in combat earned their respect. When he finally realized the difference between the Black Eagle Detachment and its personnel in comparison with conventional units, he also learned to understand the men in this unique new unit to which he had been assigned. Gordon backed off regulation behavior and displayed another side of his leadership talents. He successful acceptance was undeniable when he, like the old detachment sergeant, began to be called "Top" by the men.

The military intelligence chores were handled by a Cherokee Indian from Oklahoma. Sergeant First Class Jack Galchaser was a good family man despite being called "Horny" by the other Black Eagles; they just figured any guy named Galchaser would be a real stud. But a wife and three children waited for him back home, and despite the temptation to chase the many loose women available, Horny stayed faithful to his wife Betty Jean. He was six feet, two inches tall and weighed in at a rock-hard one hundred and ninety-eight pounds. Besides being well versed in all phases of combat intelligence, he was cross-trained as a communications man. He had been in the army ten years.

Petty Officer Second Class Fred Jackson, from the Navy SEALs, was in charge of communications. Nicknamed "Sparks," he'd just finished his second four-year hitch and reenlisted only a few weeks prior to his assignment to the Black Eagles.

Another SEAL, Chief Petty Officer Claude "Popeye" Jenkins, was in charge of demolitions. He appeared to be much older than his thirty-five years of age because he was bald, with only a sparse bit of gray hair around the sides of his head. Although heavyset, he was extremely agile and in excellent physical condition.

The United States Marine Corps had donated the

detachment supply sergeant. Staff Sergeant Liam O'Quinn was reputed to be the best scrounger of material in Southeast Asia. It was said that if "Lightfingers" O'Quinn couldn't get it, it didn't exist. Besides his passion for making sure the Black Eagles were well equipped, Lightfingers liked to eat. His tendency for becoming overweight had been kept in check, first by his service in Force Recon of the USMC, and now by the physical demands of fighting in this special detachment. His fondness for food was so great that if his nickname wasn't already "Lightfingers," it would most certainly have been "Garbage Can."

Staff Sergeant Calvin Culpepper helped Popeye Jenkins with the demolitions chores. A tall, husky black man, Calvin could set off a block of C-4 explosive under a silver dollar and get back seventy-five cents in change.

The two weapons experts were both foreigners. Staff Sergeant Tom Newcomb had been assigned from the Australian Army's crack SAS unit. Tommy was a master craftsmen with *every* type of modern infantry weapon in existence. His partner was Master Sergeant Chun Kim, an expert in infantry weapons, whose home was the ROK marine corps. Kim had collapsed from heatstroke during the unit's last mission. Although that had not been his fault — he had only recently arrived in Vietnam and had yet to become acclimated to the steamy heat — this tough Korean marine felt disgraced by the episode. He decided to make up for this loss of face by fighting particularly hard on the next mission.

The medic of the detachment was a regular mother hen named Malcomb McCorckel. This sergeant first class had a dozen years in the service and was affectionately known as "Malpractice" by the other Black Eagles.

An inch under six feet tall, Malpractice had a pleasant face and a soft voice that went along with his genuine concern over the medical condition of the detachment. He constantly hovered over them making sure they took their salt tablets when necessary, and that all sanitary conditions and facilities were up to par. Although the men grumbled over his ministrations, they did so with good humor. Each and every one knew that the medic would crawl through hell itself to pull them to safety if they ever became casualities. And he was pretty handy with either an M-16 or an AK-47.

The final member of the Black Eagles was sergeant (sometimes) Archie Dobbs who had a weakness for women, booze, and pot. His seven years in the army had been turbulent ones which included a couple of stints in post stockades and periods of running up and down the ranks from private to sergeant. A husky, compact man in excellent physical condition, Archie Dobbs's one saving grace was his ability as a scout and tracker. His skill with map and compass had made the difference between survival and destruction during both missions he had been on with the Black Eagles.

These were the men who had been virtually imprisoned in an army Special Forces B Camp by the CIA case officer Chuck Fagin. After two extremely hairy missions they were in bad need of some change and diversion through an extended period of R&R. But not only were they not to be allowed any leave time, the fates—and the authorities—were drawing up another mission behind enemy lines for them.

CHAPTER THREE

Archie Dobbs walked down the steps into the dark interior of the Black Eagles Detachment's bunker. He threaded his way through the items of equipment and other personal debris littering the small area until he reached Master Sergeant Duncan Gordon's bunk. The team sergeant, his eyes closed and mouth open, snored softly in the close heat of the quarters.

"Hey, Top," Archie said shaking him.

Gordon snorted and turned over.

"Hey, Top!" Archie said louder.

The NCO yawned in his sleep and continued to slumber.

"Hey, TOP!" Archie yelled as loud as he could.

Gordon snorted and opened his eyes. He looked around sleepily. "What?" Then his eyes focused on Archie. "Yeah?"

"You gotta come with me, Top," Archie said. "Our beer ration is all fucked up."

The ominous ring in Archie's voice, coupled with the potential disaster of his words, snapped the detachment's senior noncommissioned officer completely awake in one millisecond. "What the hell do you mean our beer ration is all fucked up?"

"Me and Horny and Malpractice went over to pick it up, and the base camp supply sergeant said our's wasn't there," Archie explained. "So I rushed back here to get you."

Gordon, clad in OD issue shorts, sat up and slipped his sockless feet into the jungle boots on the floor beside his bunk. "Where's Lightfingers?"

"I don't know," Archie said. "I looked for him first, but couldn't find him. So it's up to you to square things away for us, Top."

Gordon slapped his boonie hat on his head and clomped toward the exit in his untied footgear. "Nobody better be screwing around with our beer ration."

"Right, Top," Archie agreed trailing after him.

The pair walked across the camp under the broiling afternoon sun. It was a lethargic time of day when the heat settled over the land like a heavy, invisible blanket. It was also during these daylight hours that security could be relaxed a good deal. During daylight the surrounding countryside belonged to the counterinsurgency forces of the Americans and South Vietnamese. Only after dark, when even the brightest full moon couldn't penetrate the thick tangle of jungle, did the Viet Cong make their moves — and, during those hours, the world belonged to them.

In the center of camp, protected under coverings of sandbags, logs, packed earth and sheet iron, the area quartermaster and ordnance officer had established their supply dumps. Access was facilitated by the proximity of the camp's airstrip as well as a well-maintained helicopter landing pad located on the premises. This was the object of Master Sergeant Gordon's determined march. When he arrived there, he went straight down into the QM side and barged into the kingdom of Sergeant First Class Raúl Ortega, the Special Forces supply sergeant.

Horny Galchaser and Malpractice McCorckel were waiting there. "Howdy, Top," they greeted him.

"Hi," Gordon said. He spotted Ortega over by his desk behind the crude plank counter that divided him and his crew from the lesser beings that drew equipment from his supply staff. "Hey, Ortega."

The supply sergeant looked up from his paperwork. "Hi, Sergeant Gordon. What can I do for you?"

"We want to draw our beer rations," Gordon said.

"Hey!" Ortega's voice was angry. He got out of his chair and walked up to the counter. "I just tole these three guys that I ain't got any beer for you. None came in."

Gordon glanced past him at the cases of Budweiser stacked in the rear of the bunker. "It looks to me like it got here all right."

"That ain't yours." Ortega insisted. "That's the requisition for the B Team and the three A Teams in garrison right now. As soon as their guys show up I'm gonna issue it to 'em."

"Check your paperwork again," Gordon said. "You know damned well our supply man Lightfingers wouldn't screw up. Especially when it comes to drawing our beer."

Ortega shrugged. "Well, Sergeant Gordon, from all appearances, Lightfingers O'Quinn has let you down. You guys are SOL — Shit Out of Luck."

"Bullshit!" Gordon exclaimed. "I'm not playing any silly games about this. We're out of beer and that's the name of the game." He motioned to Archie, Horny, and Malpractice. "Go get three cases each."

"Just a fucking minute!" Ortega said menacingly. "The first asshole that comes across that counter gets a knuckle sandwich." The supply sergeant was short, but he was muscular and had once been a professional boxer in Los Angeles. Because he had fought in the ring for a living he had been kept out of the U.S. Army's fight program which was strictly for amateurs.

"Let the A Teams get their beer later," Gordon said.

"Bullshit! They're out too," Ortega said. He glared at Archie Dobbs who stood closest to the counter. "This here's my turf on this side, Dobbs. You stick your nose in here and it gets broke."

Archie shrugged. "My team sergeant says for me to get three cases of beer, so I get three cases." He hopped up on the counter and swung his legs over the side. As soon as he dropped to the floor, Ortega made his move.

The Mexican-American led with his left and peppered Archie's face with several lightning-fast jabs; then he brought his right around in an explosive hook that sent the Black Eagle staggering off to one side. Ortega followed this up with another hook, this one with his left. He ended this pugilistic display with a right upper-cut.

Archie's head snapped back and he sat down.

Ortega picked him up and slid him across the counter, sending the unconscious man crashing to the floor on the other side.

Several other Special Forces men walked into the supply room just in time to see Archie's ignominious ejection from Ortega's private territory. "What the fuck's going on?" one asked.

"These bastards are trying to steal your beer," Ortega said.

The Green Beret, a staff sergeant named Sorensen, was a rugged-looking Scandinavian type out of Minnesota. He immediately took serious exception to the Black Eagles' designs on the brew meant for his own outfit's consumption. "Hey, Gordon, lighten up, huh?"

"Look, Sorensen, there's been some fuck-up and Ortega says we got no beer," Gordon said. "Well, there is no way in hell we're going to buy that shit. There's beer there. I say it's ours and we're going to take it."

"Yeah?" Sorensen snarled, pushing his face up to Gordon's. "I say it *ain't* your's, and you *ain't* gonna take it."

Gordon smiled. "Sergeant Sorensen, I'm terribly upset about your apparent lack of cooperation. Gee whiz! It's downright disappointing."

Then he hit Sorensen so hard that the Minnesotan back-pedaled halfway up the same steps he had only recently descended.

The nearest Special Forces trooper responded to this assault on his buddy with a hard blow to Gordon's head. He used the heel of his hand, slamming the master sergeant just above his left ear. Gordon bounced against Horny, and both crashed into the counter.

Malpractice leaped across his fallen friends and drove his fist into the attacker's jaw, dropping him like a pole-axed bull. By this time Archie Dobbs had gotten to his feet and joined the Black Eagles' medic in his assault. The small area around the door turned into a battle royal as Gordon and Horny, having untangled themselves and stood again, joined in.

Raúl Ortega leaped up on his counter and bellowed out like an enraged coyote. Filled with a lust for fighting, he had all but forgotten the original reason for the conflict as he dove into the swirling, close-packed group of brawlers. He began punching at anyone near him with indiscriminate, happy abandon.

The small riot quickly drew attention from others and numerous members of the garrison piled into the disturbance as grunts, groans, yells, and the sound of fists smashing into flesh erupted from the melee.

Most didn't know what the brawl was about. It just seemed like a good idea to join in—a way, more or less, to pass a rather dull afternoon.

Several officers finally arrived on the scene and dove in to separate the combatants. It took them fifteen hard, sweating minutes, but they finally gained control of the situation. When silence once again reigned in the supply bunker, there were no less than fifteen bruised, bleeding men panting and gasping in the compressed heat.

A stern-looking captain, obviously upset with the brawl, glared at the offenders. "Now who started—"

He was interrupted by the sudden appearance of Lightfingers O'Quinn, the Black Eagles' supply sergeant. He glanced around at the group of fighters until he spotted Master Sergeant Gordon. "Hey, Top, I been lookin' all over for you. I got a special requisition of beer that's just come in. The chopper's over at our landing pad. Can you get some guys to give me a hand unloading it?"

"Sure, Lightfingers," Gordon said cheerfully through his swollen lips. "But isn't that any of ours there behind the counter?"

"No, Top," Lightfingers answered. "I been workin' on some contacts of mine and got some Coors. That's your favorite, ain't it?"

"You bet!" Top said. He turned and nodded to Ortega. "Hey, looks like our suds have just come in. See you later."

"Sure thing, Sergeant Gordon," Ortega answered with a smile. "Any time I can do anything for you guys in the future, just let me know."

"You bet." Gordon signaled to Archie, Horny, and Malpractice. "C'mon, you guys. Let's go give Lightfingers some help with the brew."

The captain, who had started to berate the brawlers, stared in gape-mouthed confusion as the Black Eagles nodded politely to the men they had just been trying to beat to a pulp, then they scampered happily after their team sergeant.

The young ARVN lieutenant dozed fitfully in the cab of the duece-and-a-half truck. The vehicle in which he rode was part of a small convoy that had left Danang several hours previously.

Now, traveling north on Highway 1, they had just come through the rugged hill country and had reached the flats that would make the traveling easier.

The cargo in the string of vehicles was human. It consisted of young ARVN soldiers, who had just completed basic training. They were packed tightly into the backs of the trucks. The rookies had been assigned to the security garrison at the Hué.

The going had been extremely slow due to security precautions. The convoy halted periodically so that a squad of engineer troops, equipped with mine detector devices, could be sent forward to sweep the road to avoid the unpleasantness of having a truck or two blown up by explosives buried in the road. And, during the trip through the hills, there had been the danger of ambush to contend with too. But that peril was gone since they had reached the open country. The Viet Cong had no desire to spring an attack in daylight when there was not much concealment available to them.

The lieutenant opened his eyes every so often to look around, then allowed himself to slip back into the uncomfortable dozing he had been trying to enjoy. The night before had been one of wild revelry in the battalion officers club, and he had drunk heavily and long. When he'd reported for convoy duty he had come directly from the party, thus he'd had no sleep in more than twenty-four hours.

Suddenly his driver called out to him, the young man's insistent voice penetrating through the haze of sleep. *"Trung Úy! Trung Úy!"*

The lieutenant, irritated, sat up. *"Chuyen gi vay?* What's the matter?"

"There are some troops ahead in the road, *Trung Úy,"* the driver said.

The lieutenant peered intently through the haze of the afternoon heat. "Big fellows. Must be *nguroi Auh.*" As they slowed and drew closer, he could see that they were, indeed, Americans. One of the GIs signaled for them to stop. The Vietnamese convoy, per standard practice, remained spread out.

When the American approached the truck it was obvious he was an officer. "Hello," he said. "You speak English?"

The lieutenant nodded. "A little . . . yes . . . a little.

How do you do?"

"I am fine," the American answered. "My name is Captain Jones."

"I am fine too, thank you, Capitaine Jones," the ARVN officer said. He could speak French better than English and had used that language's word for captain. "I am Lieutenant Han. You want with me something?"

The American spoke slowly, deliberately, "You wait here, okay? My men saw VC off the road"—he pointed—"there. We look for them for a while. When it is clear, then you go. Okay?"

"Sure. Okay," Lieutenant Han said.

"You be here for one hour maybe," Captain Jones told him. "Maybe your soldiers want to rest by trucks, hey?"

"Good idea," the lieutenant said. He opened the door and dropped to the side of the road. He yelled orders down to the other three trucks. The drivers responded to his instructions by driving close and parking bumper to bumper just behind the officer's own vehicle.

The South Vietnamese troops, happy for this opportunity to stretch their legs, gratefully climbed over the backs of the tailgates and jumped down to the ground. Most immediately took advantage of the opportunity to urinate and relieve their bladders and kidneys which had been bounced around for the previous few hours by the rough ride.

When all had attended to their bodily functions, they gathered on the road side of the convoy to watch the Americans. The big fellows didn't seem in much of a hurry. They had spread themselves out in a skirmish line facing out into the empty flats, apparently making ready to move forward in their search for guerrillas.

The American officer, still standing beside Han, lit a

cigarette. "My men will start out pretty soon."

The lieutenant nodded. "Sure. Sure." He looked at the Yanks with professional curiosity. They were approximately two-platoon strength. It seemed curious to him; this was a most unusual field organization for American troops. And there was something else too. "Ah! You no have the Negro with you?"

"Pardon me?" Jones asked.

"No black mans in your unit. I always see black mans when I see American soldiers," Lieutenant Han said.

"No. We have none," the Captain said. He offered his hand. "My men and I go look for VC. We come back and tell you when it is safe. Good-bye."

Han saluted. "Good-bye, *Capitaine*."

Captain Jones walked out to where his men waited for him. He walked through their line to the other side. Then suddenly he hollered out, *"Achtung! Drehen und schissend!"*

The troops whirled, bringing their weapons to bear on the startled South Vietnamese. The heavy staccato of automatic fire ripped through the still afternoon air as the bullets stitched the closely packed ARVN. They collapsed under the onslaught. One young soldier, panic-stricken and wild with fear, stupidly tried to climb back up into the back of his truck. Several bullets smacked into his back and he tumbled down to land on top of his dead comrades.

The blood ran from the bodies in thick rivulets that coursed under the trucks and down the slanted roadway to the soil off the macadam.

Finally the captain yelled another order. *Aufhören schiessend!"*

The silence that followed was nearly as startling as the

initial explosion of gunfire.

The captain, with his men following, walked up to the pile of victims that lay around the tires of the vehicles. He pulled some bodies aside and found Lieutenant Han. The ARVN officer, though badly wounded, was still conscious.

Han, a crimson stream coming from his mouth, stared up in disbelieving horror at the captain who stood over him. "Why? Why?"

"Because you are South Vietnamese swine," the captain said with a cold smile.

Han closed his eyes and braced for the bullet he expected to be fired into his head. But the only sound he heard was that of the heavy tread of boots walking away. He opened his eyes and raised his head as best he could.

Han saw the Americans, now in column formation, calmly walking away from the road to disappear into the surrounding countryside.

CHAPTER FOUR

When Major Robert Falconi returned to the base camp after his visit to Saigon, he couldn't help but notice the battered features of Top Gordon, Archie Dobbs, Henry Galchaser, and Malpractice McCorckel.

But he made only shallow inquiries into the matter. After learning the injuries were sustained in an altercation involving the beer issue, his only question was to find out if the matter had been properly resolved. When he was informed it had, Falconi put the episode out of his mind. He was far too concerned with the upcoming Operation Asian Blitzkrieg to become involved in minor matters of scraps.

And, besides, Major Falconi was frankly surprised that none of the tightly confined Black Eagles had committed murder as of yet.

Falconi had brought the OPPLAN (Operations Plan) as drawn up by Chuck Fagin and his cohorts back in SOG headquarters. It was now time for the major and his men to convert this thick document into the OPORD (Operations Order). This would be done by taking the information, requirements and general dope in the OPPLAN and passing the data out among the members of the detachment so they could give their attention to those things that pertained to their particular areas of responsibility and expertise.

They would then rewrite all this and return it to Major Falconi. The commander, with Master Sergeant Gordon, would collate and further arrange this into annexes to form the OPORD. This would be the final document that directed the Black Eagles on the where, when, and how of their mission.

Much paperwork in the military is unmitigated bullshit. Other types, like OPPLANS and OPORDS, are terribly essential because of the need for every man in the outfit to know *exactly* what the hell is going on. In the deadly world of the Black Eagles, ignorance was definitely not bliss, as per the old cliché — it was certain failure.

And a failed mission meant men died.

Less than twenty-four hours after the Falcon's return, the bunker had been turned into a study hall. The clacking of GI portable typewriters filled the compact area as each man labored on his particular project. Now and then an individual would stop long enough for a quick conference and an exchange of ideas with another; then he'd return to his machine and once again get at the chore of grinding out the words he would soon dispense to the others.

This was part of the mission known as Isolation — and the term could be taken literally. The Black Eagles were isolated, even to the point of having guards posted around their area of the camp to keep intruders — accidental or otherwise — away from them. The only time one of the men was allowed to leave the bunker would be to tend to business which could not be taken care of within the confines of their small world. This was Light-fingers O'Quinn most of the time. As supply man he had to personally see to the physical acquisition of needed items of equipment.

And he had to have the opportunity to steal things too. A good supply sergeant does not live by proper requisitions alone.

Within seventy-two hours the OPORD was ready. Thus, the next phase of Isolation began: the Briefback.

The bunker was turned into a small, impromptu the-ater. Falconi addressed the gathered detachment in a brief introduction of the affair.

"We're running short of time, guys," he told them. "So let's get into this without further ado." He made sure each and every man was giving his full attention. "Our mission on Operation Asian Blitzkrieg is to locate an unknown military unit thought to be of approximately double-platoon size. This outfit is committing atrocities while disguised as American troops. Once they are found, the aforementioned unit will be destroyed or captured—with a big emphasis on the latter. Top will now cover the execution phase of the OPORD."

Master Sergeant Duncan Gordon went to the front of the room. "Okay, troops, here's the time elements, and I want to emphasize most strongly that they'll have to be followed *exactly*. We're coordinating through three serv-ices: army, air force, and navy."

"But not necessarily in that order of importance, right, Top?" Popeye Jenkins, a navy man, asked.

"That's all a matter of opinion I guess," Top said with a smile. Then he continued. "We leave out of here tomorrow night at 2000 hours aboard the regular supply plane's return flight. Any casual observer seeing us get aboard will assume we're going to Saigon for R&R."

"What's that?" Archie Dobbs asked.

"What? R&R?" Top inquired.

"Yeah. It seems I heard the term somewhere way, way back in my army career," Archie said. "It always gave me a contented feeling, as I recall."

"I'm not sure myself," Top Gordon said, going along with the scout's irony.

"I think it means Rest and Recreation, whatever that is," Malpractice McCorckel volunteered sarcastically.

"I think you're right," Top said. "But we're digressing, gentlemen. Let's get back to our airplane. Instead of flying its usual return trip, the aircraft will take us to Vung Tau way down south."

"But not way down south in the Land o' Dixie, right, Top?" Horny Galchaser asked.

"Not hardly," Gordon answered. "We'll actually be on the air base there that's located on the coast. A pair of seven-man rafts will be provided for us to row out for a rendezvous with the USS *Perch*. I'm sure just about all of us are familiar with that sub. It's a World War II job that's been converted for troop-carrying missions."

Lightfingers O'Quinn, the marine, spoke up. "That's my second home. I used to go out on it a lot when I was stationed at Camp Del Mar in Pendleton."

"Well, your second home is going to carry us around the Horn—so to speak—to our disembarkation point in the west of Cape Tourane. That area is crawling with informers, double agents, spies, and assholes. And each has a direct line to Hanoi, Peking, and/or Moscow. If we're spotted, not only will the entire local population be aware of our arrival, but so will the hierarchy of the Communist world. So we'll leave the sub in our trusty rafts — during the dark of night — and row to the beach. After moving into the bush, we'll stow the things and begin our Search-and-Destroy mission." Top paused. "I want to emphasize one thing, men. We stay there until the mission is accomplished."

"Or we're all dead," Archie Dobbs added.

"Right," Top agreed, "When the job is done, we'll withdraw to Danang and be flown back here."

"What's the surf conditions on the infiltration beach," Lightfingers asked.

"Moderate to heavy swells," Top answered. "So the guys acting as coxswains are going to have to work hard to keep those boats straight in line with the shore. Or else there's going to be some capsizing that'll result in lost equipment — and possibly personnel too."

Calvin Culpepper held up his hand, "Let's get back to the R&R question for a minute, Top. Are we gonna get any after this shit's all done?"

Falconi interjected. "You *will* have R&R. Count on it! I'm giving you my word we'll all be back in Saigon at the termination of Operation Asian Blitzkrieg."

A cheer broke from the assembled detachment.

Top Gordon grinned. "And on that happy note I shall relinquish the floor to Horny Galchaser for the intelligence portion of the briefing."

Horny was almost apologetic. "It looks like I got the easiest job in the briefing — except for engineering maybe — because we don't have any intelligence. Or at least not much. All we know is that a group of Caucasians in American Army uniforms have been running around in that area committing atrocities and war crimes. We haven't got the slightest idea who the bastards are. They could be anybody—even American deserters or turncoats."

"Are there that many of our guys missing or unaccounted for?" Malpractice asked.

"Yeah, though most are either legitimate MIAs or are wrapped up in the narcotics crime scene."

Calvin Culpepper stood up. "I know who they are," the black man said. "The Klu Klux Klan! Who else?"

Horny laughed. "Hell, Calvin, you may be right. I'll add that to the list of suspicious characters they gave me. It's been confirmed by an ARVN lieutenant who was among the last victims that there were no Negroes in the group. He thought this was rather odd."

"Hell!" Calvin snorted. "They ain't only killers, they're prejudiced too. I tole you they was the Klan."

"You could have hit the nail on the head again," Horny said. "But it's been thought they could be eastern Europeans out to discredit American involvement in Southeast Asia. White men dressed in our duds could move among people not too familiar with English—or the American brand of it—and be very convincing as GI's. We'll fill in the holes when we catch up with 'em. And that is a point I want to emphasize: G-2 at SOG wants prisoners. So if you can avoid killing any of the bastards, try to pull a Frank Buck and bring 'em back alive. The kind of intelligence a guy like that could provide would be priceless." He paused. "Since I didn't have any information, I know there ain't any questions. So I'll let Lightfingers give the dope on supply."

Lightfingers was also brief. "We'll draw all boat gear from the navy down at Vung Tau. There'll be no fancy stuff used on this one, just standard issue. But I'll have an inspection to make sure all your field gear is there and what you have is up to par. Report any shortages to me after this briefing and I'll get right on drawing some new stuff or replacements for worn and busted up items. We won't be taking in too much with us. There'll be re-supply drops per SOP outta Danang when we need them. They say there'll be some special goodies available if we run into any unusual needs, so it looks like we're fat and happy on this trip anyway." It was typical of Lightfingers not to ask if there were any questions. He didn't like to talk. "Sparks will give us the commo briefing."

Sparks Jackson, the navy SEAL radioman, went to the front of the small room. "I still got my trusty AN/PRC-41 from the last operation. The call sign for us is Black Eagle on a frequency of three-two-five. That'll be for contact with the Powers-That-Be in Danang. Inter-detachment commo will be on three Prick-Sixes. I didn't strain my imagination for call signs. Falcon is *Falcon,* Fire Team Alpha is *Alpha* and Fire Team Bravo is *Bravo.* If nobody's got questions I'll let Popeye have the floor."

Chief Petty Officer Popeye Jenkins didn't even bother to stand up. "As of this moment there's no demolitions or engineer work in the OPPLAN. If any comes up me and Calvin will handle it on the fly. Now here's Malprac-tice with the medical stuff."

They waited as Malpractice McCorckel threaded his way through the assembled troops and went to the front of the room. "We all suffered from heatstroke on the last mission, so I don't have to emphasize the problem. I tell you guys this before every mission, and I'm telling you again — take the salt tablets. Drink plenty of water and do little things to help yourself out. Tie a wet bandana around your neck, or soak your boonie hat in a handy creek or stream whenever there's a chance and wear it that way. The evaporation will cool your noggins down. Ever'body has enough sense not to try to pet any cobras you run into. You're all familiar with edible plants, so if you see one that is unknown to you, I would advise you not to eat it. Treat insect bites promptly and avoid scratching them. Come to me for cuts and abrasions, they'll infect quickly out there without proper treatment. I'll be checking feet periodically for blisters. If you get one, come and see me. That's it, guys. Just use common sense." Malpractice nodded to the big Australian SAS sergeant. "Now Tommy Newcomb will enlighten us in regard to mission weaponry."

"Right, mates," Tommy said. "We'll, of course, be going in with our M-16s. Ammo is no problem. Additional rounds will be handled through Lightfingers and his resupply. There'll be no heavy weapons support such as mortars or recoilless rifles. But both myself and Kim will be carrying M-79 grenade launchers, and you'll each be given four grenades to carry on your harness. If it becomes an absolute necessity, there is a possibility, though quite remote, that we'll be able to have air strikes." He paused for questions, but there were none. "And now, lads, back to our great and fearless leader."

"Okay, gentlemen," Falconi said. "Before I break us down into teams, I think it's time to hear from Dinky Dow." He motioned to the ARVN officer. "What's your particular briefing on this operation?"

Dinky Dow leaped to his feet and screamed, *"Kick ass!"*

The Black Eagles cheered and clapped, then settled down as Falconi continued his spiel.

"I'll post the mission organization. After you've read it, get back to work and prepare to tap each other's minds. Questions?"

Since there were none, he took the paper he'd typed up and tacked it to the cork bulletin board mounted on the bunker's south wall.

COMMAND AND SIGNAL
Maj. Robert Falconi, Commander
PO2c. Sparks Jackson, Radio Operator

FIRE TEAM ALPHA
1st Lt. Dinky Dow, Team Leader
Sgt. Archie Dobbs, Scout
S. Sgt. Tommy Newcomb, Grenadier
Sfc. Horny Galchaser
CPO Popeye Jenkins

FIRE TEAM BRAVO
M. Sgt. Top Gordon, Team Leader
Sfc. Malcomb McCorckel, Medic
M. Sgt. Chun Kim, Grenadier
S. Sgt. Lightfingers O'Quinn
S. Sgt. Calvin Culpepper

Each member noted his particular assignment, then went back to study the brand new OPORD.

Their next activity would be the phase of the Brief-back that had been Falconi's own idea for rounding off the mission preparation. In this phase, they would do more than simply recite their own particular part of the operation. After a detailed perusal of the operation's execution they would be expected to give the full and complete details on everyone else's job and responsibility.

51

In the event a man died, somebody — *anybody* — had to be able to expertly fill in whatever gap he left. This not only insured the success of the endeavor, but it made sure there was no weak link in the Black Eagle chain. It was all part of the Three Bs of this type outfit:

Brains, Brawn, and Bravery.

CHAPTER FIVE

Rolf Stahler was born in an *SS Stä*rke durch Freude Lager — SS Strength through Joy Camp — located in the eastern part of Germany in the year of 1934.

His mother was a pale blond attractive young girl named Lotte Müller, whose blue eyes and rather athletic body fit her into Heinrich Himmler's description of the ideal Aryan woman.

She had been chosen as a inhabitant of the camp not only because of these physical attributes, but also because she had expressed a willingness to follow, without question, the philosophies and dictates of National Socialism. Another important criteria she met, was the fact Lotte Müller was willing to bear the baby of any SS trooper chosen by the authorities to father it.

The particular trooper selected to mate with her was a robust, blond Adonis *SS-Scharführer* (sergeant) named Dieter Stahler. At the time Stahler was twenty-four years old and a veteran of the street campaigns conducted by the Nazi party during Adolph Hitler's ascent to power. He had proven his loyalty and devotion through numerous brawls in which he'd conducted himself fearlessly and fiercely to the extent that when Hitler decided to expand his personal bodyguard—known as the *Schutzstaffel*—into an army to be literally owned and financed by the Nazi party, Dieter Stahler became a member of that select force's most elite regiment: *Liebstandarte Adolf Hitler.* They formed what was to become the core of the dreaded *Waffen-SS,* a hard-fighting corps that gave no quarter in combat—and asked for none.

These fanatically loyal soldiers were among the first allowed access to the racially pure maidens who waited, with sly smiles and large breasts, to be impregnated by SS soldiers. This was all part of SS-Reichsführer Heinrich Himmler's program of producing a race of pure Aryan warriors for Germany's plan to conquer the world. Within twenty-years, Himmler expected every continent on this earth to tremble beneath the crash of these SS Supermen's jackboots.

Dieter Stahler and Lotte Müller were introduced at a party in the camp. This rather pleasant social event was designed to put the young people at ease and in a good mood before they would withdraw to special cabins to begin the coupling. Any romantic feelings the girls might have had faded when they learned a sobering fact. The SS troopers about to mount them had formed a pool into which each had contributed twenty-five reichsmarks. The first man to impregnate his mating partner would take the pot.

The evening was marked by music, good food, and plenty of beer and schnapps. After midnight the couples began to drift away from the party in order to get on with the planned process of producing babies for *der Vaterland.*

Lotte's experience with Dieter was not too pleasant. He had never had a regular girl friend before. All his previous love-making had been done with prostitutes, although once or twice he'd had a drunken rendezvous with a barmaid after an evening of heavy drinking following a Nazi party rally. And his year as both a street brawler and barracks dweller did nothing to enhance any tenderness in his make-up.

Drunk and horny, SS-Scharführer Stahler ripped away Lotte's maidenhead in a pushing, grinding, pumping ordeal that left her bleeding and weeping on the bed. After ejaculating his Aryan seed into her abused vagina, the trooper rolled over and fell into a deep sleep brought on by both the physical relief he had just enjoyed and the large amounts of alcohol he had consumed previously.

Lotte Müller bore up under these sexual assaults for a week before Stahler had to report back to his regiment. When, at the end of the month, she didn't get her period, she sighed with hope. A few weeks later it was determined she was pregnant and the girl nearly wept with relief that Dieter Stahler would not be returning to her bed. Some other poor girl could now spread her legs to the crude assault SS-Scharführer Stahler would visit upon her.

Lotte settled into the pampered life of pregnancy in the camp. She performed no chores—in fact, the girl was waited on hand and foot by young women who had not conceived or who had yet to try—and she ate well, gained weight as she prepared for the day she would deliver.

The baby came in late winter. Lotte named him Rolf after her favorite older brother. The child gave every evidence of being racially pure. Light wisps of blond hair danced across his tiny head, and his blue eyes watered with every lusty yell he gave in his seemingly insatiable demand for his mother's milk. Lotte held the infant to her breast and nursed him, her status in this community of breeders now upgraded even more.

Rolf Stahler — given his father's name through official SS decree — grew up with others like himself in the camp. By the time he was five, the youngster had two more half brothers and a half sister (none of the Strength-through-Joy girls had babies with the same man). Also, during this period, Germany had charged across Poland's frontiers, and World War II was in the making.

Those early years were heady ones for the German public. Newspapers and radio reported victory after victory as Europe was swept over by the *Wehrmacht* and the *Waffen-SS* with the *Luftwaffe* covering them from the air. All Germans expected an armistice so they could get back to high living at the expense of the conquered nations.

But they didn't reckon on Great Britain's bulldoglike tenacity and bravery in resisting German aims. The culmination of this resistance came in the Battle of Britain when the Royal Air Force defeated the *Luftwaffe* in explosive aerial duels high above the troubled earth.

It was a harbinger of things to come.

The German armed forces had now taken on the Soviet Union, and the Americans — after the dastardly attack by the Japanese at Pearl Harbor — were mad as hell at all three of the Axis nations. Thus Germany and its Japanese and Italian allies were about to have the full strength and resources of the free world descend upon them like demons from the bowels of Hades.

Even Russia, the slave state, had help from the Allies. The master murderer Stalin saw the opportunity not only to get aid in stopping the German invasion, but possibly to involve the United States and Britain in unwittingly furthering his dreams of world conquest.

Meanwhile Rolf Stahler served in the Hitler Youth and continued to grow during the difficult war years. He was a blond, husky youngster who, with his fellow super*kinder,* ate better than the average German child whose diet was curtailed by wartime rationing. His mother, fading emotionally because of her life as a state breeder, became less important to him as the Nazi party increased its influence over his thinking. Thoroughly indoctrinated, Rolf was the National Socialist of the future, faithful, strong, and even at a tender age, a rather well-trained soldier. Part of the school day in the camp was devoted to military skills in this program of producing the future leaders of the world.

But that world was blown apart in the terrible year of 1945. The Americans and their allies were pushing in from the west. The barbarians of the Asian continent, the Soviet army, closed in relentlessly from the east, bringing wholesale slaughter, rapine, and plundering.

The German situation got so bad in those latter days of the war that even the Hitler Youth was mobilized for a last-ditch effort at thwarting defeat. Rolf Stahler, eleven years old, was handed a *panzerfaust* — a one-shot antiarmor device — and told to go out and destroy a Russian tank.

It was to the boy's credit that he performed his duty fearlessly. His *Hitlerjugend* detachment, along with a miserable group of elderly men of the desperately conceived *Volksheer,* was attached to a company of war-weary regular army veterans. Brave with the ignorance and optimism of youth, Rolf crouched in the foxhole he had dug hastily and awaited the advancing Russians.

Within a scant two hours the first Soviets appeared. The T-34 tanks rumbled ominously toward them. Rolf, being well trained, waited with his *Panzerfaust,* and took aim at the correct range. He squeezed the trigger and the small rocket streaked out, striking the tank at the bottom of the turret.

The armored vehicle abruptly stopped and smoke immediately poured out of its observation slits. A couple of seconds later the survivors of the crew leaped from the back escape hatch. But nearby German troops raked them with their MG-42 machine guns dropping the unlucky Red soldiers into tattered heaps.

Watching the Russians die proved a vicarious thrill for young Rolf. He found a great pleasure in watching them twitch under the impact of the 9-millimeter slugs before collapsing in death.

But the tactical situation did not continue in the Germans' favor and they were forced to withdraw. Two days later, armed with a Mauser rifle taken from the corpse of a dead countryman, Rolf killed his first human beings with well-placed shots. He found this much more fun than watching others shoot them.

But after only a scant two weeks in combat, Rolf and others were surrounded by some determined Russians. Out of ammunition and rations, and fatigued beyond relief, the Germans surrendered.

Thus, Rolf Stahler, eleven years of age, ended World War II as a prisoner of war.

Most German soldiers captured by the Russians

faced certain death. If not massacred outright by the Soviet front-line troops, they were shipped back to the rear where they faced more than ten years in POW cages located in the remotest and least habitable parts of Stalin's empire.*

Young Rolf Stahler's age came to his aid when he became a prisoner. During the war Josef Stalin had forged plans to bring a great part of Europe under his domination. He foresaw no hindrance from the Allied powers. The Russian generalissimo figured if they were dumb enough to help him in the struggle against the Germans, they were probably dumb enough not to hinder his postwar dream of enslaving millions of eastern Europeans after the war.

Stalin needed help in order to forge the chains he planned to use to strangle vast areas of territory. There weren't enough trustworthy Russians to do the job. But, Stalin surmised, if he followed Hitler's example and grabbed the youth, he would soon have a new generation of Communists that would obey, without question or protest, all directives and orders from Moscow.

Rolf Stahler then found himself in a situation where an unfamiliar political philosophy was being pounded into his head. In a special camp for former Hitler Youth, he learned a different brand of socialism. Unlike the Nazis, the Russians did not preach a national brand of that system; rather they emphasized an *inter*national

*In 1955, the Soviet Union announced that all surviving German POWs had been returned. But, like most Russian claims, this one is impossible to substantiate. The list of German soldiers missing and unaccounted for while in Soviet captivity makes a long, thick file.

style. But it was still racist, and Stahler found that under Stalin he could hate Jews with the same abandon he had exercised while a follower of Adolf Hitler. The only difference was that Stalin's death camps were not confined to certain minorities. The Russians practiced genocide on any group of people they deemed dangerous to their causes and goals.

The Soviet Communists were equal-opportunity exterminators.

Rolf prospered well under this system. The young German was the type to follow any political system that would provide him with the opportunity to have power over other people. He demonstrated the same fanaticism for Communism that his father had for Nazism. Rolf was placed in a state school where he grew to manhood under the influence of Marxism and its militaristic and imperialistic dictates. At the age of eighteen, he took the state examinations and successfully passed them for admittance to the military academy of the *Bereitschaftpolizei* — the Alert Police.

This unit's primary missions were the investigation of and the elimination of antiregime activity. While a subordinate part of the East German People's Police the Alert Police were a power unto themselves. Trained in small-unit infantry tactics and equipped with modern Soviet weaponry, they were a force to be reckoned with.

Young Rolf, accepted as a cadet, lived the diversified life of the officer candidate. His academic education, while heavily tainted with Communist rhetoric was good enough to make him proficient in several languages including English. These stints in the classroom were broken by tours of duty in the field. By the time he had completed the course and received his commission as junior lieutenant, Rolf Stahler was a trusted, devoted Communist, utterly reliable to the Russian masters who ruled his homeland.

His physical appearance was also impressive. Tall, muscular, and displaying a blond Teutonic handsomeness, Rolf Stahler looked the part of the Prussian officer despite the leftist militarism of his background.

His service in the Alert Police was exemplary. Within five years he became an instructor in the infantry tactics section of the same academy where he had studied. He even went to the Soviet Union for various assignments designed to broaden his knowledge and usefulness to the state.

It was here he came to the pleased attention of the KGB.

Lieutenant Colonel Gregori Krashchenko, assigned to an important and sensitive positition in the KGB's military intelligence section, had supervised an exhaustive investigation of Captain Rolf Stahler. The German's career was marked by rapid promotion and glowing letters of recommendation and commendation for his "vigorous suppression of enemies of the state." Not only had Stahler organized and led raids against clandestine underground groups in East Germany, he had participated in a particularly bloody campaign against insurgents in the Ukraine during a tour of duty in the Soviet Union.

An entire Ukrainian village of defectors had fled their communal farm organization and, armed with weapons stolen from local armories, had conducted a program of guerrilla warfare that threatened to spread and get out of hand in that particularly rebellious section of the Soviet Union. Rolf, with his company of Alert Police, had been brought into the area and attached to the Russian security troops. The young East German officer had been most energetic and vigorous in his part of the fighting, to the extent that, in the final attack on the die-hard resistance fighters, he had personally spearheaded the assault which had resulted in a massacre of the survivors.

Stahler had returned to East Germany after that, but Krashchenko, who had been present during the affair, intended to keep the young officer in mind in case there would be any use for him in other undertakings. But the Russian KGB man, gradually forgot the East German officer.

Then Lieutenant Colonel Krashchenko was sent to North Vietman to take over the campaign against an unknown group of Americans who were making devastating—and embarrassing—raids deep into the Communist heartlands. Krashchenko finally identified these raiders through agents and double agents in South Vietnam. Called the Black Eagles, they were an elite fighting outfit led by an energetic and resourceful officer named Robert Mikhailovich Falconi. This man, whose mother was a Russian Jew, would be a great propaganda ploy for the Reds if he could be captured. His mother's nationality made the American a Soviet citizen under their laws. If Krashchenko could get his hands on Falconi, he would be able to use the prisoner in all sorts of ways, if only to try and convict him as a traitor to set an example for others with family connections to Russia who might have the gall to want to resist the Soviet plans for expansion and conquest.

The Black Eagles had hit a pleasure palace in North Vietnam—this was hushed up due to the obvious embarrassment and shame it could cause to the strictly moralistic Communist hierarchy—had freed internees in a secret prison camp in North Vietnam, and lastly, had destroyed the site of a nuclear power plant under construction in Laos.

Krashchenko wanted Falconi and his Black Eagles. However, although he had learned who they were, he didn't know their location. If he waited until they pulled another operation, he might miss and they would do even more damage. His best bet was to set up a ploy to draw them out into a place where he knew they would show up—then hit them with every ounce of firepower he could muster.

It was these latter thoughts that caused him to suddenly remember Captain Rolf Stahler in the East German Alert Police. He would be invaluable in neutralizing Robert Falconi. The only problem was to figure out how to utilize Stahler's natural and energetic devotion to serving the state through violence.

Then Krashchenko came up with the perfect ploy.

He would get Stahler and some of his most trusted men in the *Bereitschaftpolizei,* bring them to Southeast Asia and dress them in captured American Army uniforms. These Europeans could easily simulate being GIs among the indigenous population. By committing atrocities against the Vietnamese people, they would aid the communist cause twofold: they would generate hatred against the United States, and—more importantly—the one outfit that would be sent out to look into the situation would, without any doubt at all, be the Black Eagles.

Krashchenko set the administrative wheels of the KGB turning, and within a matter of weeks Captain

Rolf Stahler and twenty of his men were in Peking awaiting a meeting with the Russian KGB operative.

Final instructions, training, and equipping were accomplished in Red China. There had even been a rehearsal against a rebellious Mongol village to the north. These fiercely independent desert dwellers had shown a marked dislike for Mao's form of government. They not only refused to cooperate with government officials sent to chastise and guide them, these descendants of Genghis Khan's hordes had the habit of tying these interloping Peking agents behind their horses and dragging them across the hard ground of those cold northern deserts.

Rolf Stahler and his men moved into the village late at night, rousted the inhabitants, and killed them all — men, women and children — within the space of one hour.

Gregori Krashchenko, after viewing this demonstration of efficient massacre, rubbed his hands together in happy anticipation of what the East Germans would be able to accomplish in South Vietnam.

And the inevitable clash between Robert Falconi and Rolf Stahler gave all evidence of being among the bloodiest in even this fiercely developing war.

CHAPTER SIX

Major Robert Falconi, with the rest of the Black Eagles spread out single file behind him in the bowels of the submarine, ascended the ladder leading to the deck.

He shoved his rucksack and weapon through the small hatch opening above his head and followed it through. It was a dark, moonless night. The Black Eagles had been kept in a compartment with red lights to enhance their visual capabilities at night. As the others popped out of the interior of the underwater craft, the detachment commander rushed across the deck to the forward seven-man raft and set his gear inside. He took his place in the coxswain's position at the rear while Dinky Dow's Alpha Fire Team joined him.

Top Gordon, with his own Bravo Team on his heels, took the craft just to the rear. He, too, was a coxswain and he readied himself as the remainder of his small command positioned themselves.

Calvin Culpepper, the last man out, slammed the hatch cover shut. He could hear the locking wheel being rapidly spun by one of the submarine's crewmen as he took his place in the second raft. This was followed by the ominous gushing of the sub's tank filling with sea water. Then the boat slowly, but steadily sank from beneath the rafts until they were afloat. Even before the conning tower disappeared under the waves, Falconi loudly whispered the command:

"Starboard around port!"

The men on the starboard sides of the rafts paddled forward while their buddies on the port sides rowed backward. The two rafts turned toward the beach.

"Give way together!"

In well-drilled precision, the Black Eagles dipped their paddles into the sea and pulled in the direction of land. Both coxswains, keeping their voices down, called the cadence.

"Pull! Pull! Pull! Pull!"

Within a few minutes they could feel the first surges of the surf growing beneath them. Falconi and Top, each with his single paddle dipped in the sea at the sterns of the rubber boats, used the small oars as rudders as they fought to keep their individual rafts moving at direct right angles to the growing speed of the waves.

The two teams were now twenty-five yards apart. Despite this relative closeness, the surf under Top Gordon's boat was slightly different. There was a large, unseen boulder beneath the water. Although it had been worn smooth by eons of waves rushing across it, the huge stone was still large enough to effect the flow of water across it.

When the bottom of Top's raft crossed the top of the submerged obstacle, the sudden shift in the current's direction and strength caused the rubber craft to turn unexpectedly. In spite of the master sergeant's best efforts, it continued until it was broadside to the waves. A particularly large one swelled up beneath it, then curled over.

"Port around starboard!" Top commanded. But he was too late.

The following wave smacked the raft and it rapidly tilted over, spilling men and equipment into the swirling water. The only things the capsized crew were aware of as they went under were paddles and each other's legs. All expert swimmers, they stroked with the current until their feet hit the sandy bottom. Top took a quick head count and was glad to see that all had come out of the mishap without injury.

But their rucksacks and weapons were gone.

"Okay," Top said. "No sense in dogging it. Let's pull the raft into the trees and set about camouflaging it."

Falconi, with Sparks at his heels, joined them. "Everything lost, Top?"

"Looks like it, Skipper," Top said apologetically. "I don't know what the hell happened. We were zipping in with the surf and before I knew it we broached. Must've been something under the water."

"We're going to have to take time to look for your gear," Falconi said. He knew that Popeye Jenkins and Sparks Jackson, both from the Navy Seals, were the two best swimmers in the detachment. He wasted no time in assigning them the task of swimming out to search for the missing items in the surf.

Both men stripped and waded out into the waves; then they dove in and swam to the approximate spot where the raft had tipped. They repeatedly cleaved into the water, fighting the surging currents as they blindly groped at the sandy bottom in hopes of finding the rucksacks and weapons.

"Sorry, Skipper," Popeye said. "Couldn't find shit out there."

"Yeah," Sparks echoed. "There's a big-assed boulder and the current is playing all around it. That's prob'ly what spilled them guys. I guess there's an undertow — I could feel one. So it probably pulled that stuff out to deeper water."

"We could find it if we went out farther," Popeye suggested.

"Never mind," Falconi said. "We don't have the time. The longer we hang around here, the bigger the chance of getting spotted. We're going to have to get off this beach pronto and into the woods. But I sure hope none of that stuff washes ashore. It'd be a dead giveaway of our presence here." He motioned to Lightfingers. "As soon as Sparks dries off, set him up for a resupply drop. I'll pick out a DZ."

They moved away from the shoreline and into the jungle. Once they were concealed in the dense vegetation, Falconi slipped his mapcase out and studied the topographic sheet in the red glow of his flashlight.

Lightfingers O'Quinn, kneeling beside him, pointed to an open area on the map. "That looks like a good spot, Skipper."

"Right," Falconi agreed. "And it's on our line of march." He made a quick calculation. "The grid coordinates are one-zero-eight-niner-zero-one-five-two-two-five. Tonight at 2100 hours."

"Right," Lightfingers said. He hastily wrote the numbers down then checked his commo supply code. "We'll need a complete resupply for one fire team then."

Sparks was ahead of him. "Alpha-Bravo-Alpha-one-zero-eight-niner-zero-one-five-two-two-five, at 2100 hours this date, right?"

"Way to go, Sailor," Lightfingers said.

"We're in a hurry," Falconi reminded his radio operator. "Use voice."

"Aye, aye," Skipper," Sparks said. He turned on his set and spoke in a low murmur into the microphone. The request for the resupply, all previously anticipated and coded before the mission, took but a few seconds to transmit. He nodded to the Black Eagles' leader. "We're all set."

"Okay. Since the Bravos only have the .45s on their pistol belts, we'll put 'em in the middle of the Alphas. Where the hell is Archie?"

The detachment scout, who had been conversing with the men in Top Gordon's Bravo Fire Team, hurried over and reported to Falconi. "Ready to go, Skipper. Same route we figured out?"

"It'll still do," Falconi said.

Dobbs took out his compass. The azimuth he had chosen had been carefully prepared with the sliding lens covers over the instrument. He placed the longest luminous line over magnetic north, then sighted down the shorter line. "Let's get this show on the road, boys," he said.

Although formed up in a rather bizarre manner, the Black Eagles moved deeper into the jungle behind the intrepid scout.

Operation Asian Blitzkrieg, even though off to a rather shaky start, was underway.

Chuck Fagin had experienced a sense of foreboding when the call from Colonel Ngai Quang had come through.

Although it had been a simple request for an informal meeting, Fagin felt there would be a deeper, more complicated situation developing from it. He did not like Colonel Ngai one damned bit.

The colonel was a top intelligence supervisor for ARVN and had the complete trust of both the American military and diplomatic missions to South Vietnam, but Fagin's instincts screamed a warning into his subconscious at each mention or thought of the colonel.

The expected arrival of Ngai had so unnerved and angered him that Fagin was unable to tend to his other duties. He sat drumming his fingers on his desk as he anticipated the visit to his office.

The intercom buzzed, and Andrea Thuy's voice sounded in the instrument. "Mister Fagin, Colonel Ngai is here."

Fagin gritted his teeth and hesitated. But he hit the button on the communications instrument. "Send him in, please." He suddenly had a second thought. It might prove convenient sometime in the future if he had a witness to whatever happened during the next few minutes. "And you come also, please, Lieutenant Thuy."

"Yes, sir."

The door opened. Andrea preceded the Vietnamese colonel into the office. Colonel Ngai wore a fancy, tailored gabardine uniform with heavy epaulettes bearing the three stars of a colonel in the ARVN. A short, very thin man, he displayed his toothy smile and offered his hand. "How are you, Mister Fagin?"

"I'm fine, thank you, Colonel. Please sit down."

Ngai took a chair. He turned his attention to the attaché case he carried with him. After fishing out some papers from it, he handed them over to Fagin. "An official request from South Vietnamese Army Intelligence."

Fagin took the documents and glanced at them. "It'll take me a few moments to peruse all this."

"Of course," Ngai said politely. "Please take your time."

"I'll also have Lieutenant Thuy read these when I've finished," Fagin added.

"There could be no question of objection to that," Ngai said pleasantly.

It took them two and a half hours to go through the trilingual papers. They were in Vietnamese, English, and—curiously, French. The Vietnamese, after decades of colonial bureaucracy, were still not flexible enough to have eliminated their former masters' language from official paperwork.

The contents, no matter in what language, upset Fagin tremendously. Only through exerting a great deal of self-control was he able to keep his expression passive and emotionless.

When he finished he laid them down on his desk. Still poker-faced, he looked at Ngai. "Impossible."

"Pardon?"

"There is absolutely no way that I can honor this request," Fagin said.

"Perhaps you failed to note that this correspondence comes from the highest echelon of the South Vietnamese Army—and therefore, the government as well," Ngai said.

Fagin's Irish temper snapped. "I don't give a fuck if they're from God Himself! I said no, goddamn it, and I mean *no!*"

Ngai, though still smiling, displayed his own annoyance. "I'm afraid there is no question of your compliance, Mister Fagin. Although this has been termed a request, it is actually much more than that."

Andrea Thuy added her own opinion. "This is completely uncalled for and without precedent."

Ngai slowly turned toward her, his eyes narrowing with indignation. "You have been around the Americans too long, Lieutenant Thuy. You seem to have forgotten that you are not only a South Vietnamese, but also a member of your nation's armed forces."

"I am assigned to Special Operations Group," Andrea said. "And I am Mister Fagin's special staff and administrative officer. I am aware of what is helpful or a hindrance in the performance of the missions assigned to us."

"And having to keep outside bureaus completely briefed on all Black Eagle operations would be most harmful to us," Fagin added. "More people knowing about these operations will increase the very real danger of compromise."

"Of course I understand your apprehension," Ngai said, keeping his voice calm. "And I remind you that this request is limited. You are required to keep only myself informed with up-to-date briefings as well as a detailed report on the past performances of the Black Eagles. And, it goes without saying, that all future activities will also be made known to me prior to their being put into effect."

"My God, Ngai!" Fagin fumed. "You're an intelligence officer, for Chrissake! Surely you can appreciate the need for letting as few other agencies as possible know about SOG's undertakings. And anyone receiving such information must have a solid, undeniable need-to-know."

"That would be me," Ngai insisted.

"The hell it would!"

"Mister Fagin, I demand an immediate briefing and report on the current status and location of the Black Eagles which is to include a full revelation on whatever mission they've been assigned to presently," Ngai said.

"I most certainly will not!"

"Suit yourself, Mister Fagin." He turned to Andrea. "I Order you, Lieutenant Thuy, *order you* to submit a written report to my office with the information requested in these documents. Failure to do so will result in your court-martial."

"Lieutenant Thuy has correctly informed you that she is attached to SOG," Fagin reminded Ngai. "And she is under our jurisdiction until she is reassigned."

Ngai angrily stood up. "I can see to that immediately." He sneered openly at the young woman. "We are well aware that you have been having sexual relations with the Black Eagles' commander, Lieutenant. And your wanton behavior has been cause to have you pulled from active operations. Without a doubt you are heading for disgrace, a court-martial and even a prison sentence."

"That's enough! Fagin snapped. "You may leave my office, Colonel Ngai."

"This woman has performed as a prostitute at various times in the past," Ngai said.

"That's not fair!" Andrea cried. "It was in the line of duty."

Ngai ignored her, his eyes snapping back to Fagin. "Are you officially refusing to comply with the request to keep the South Vietnamese fully informed of the activities of the Black Eagles?"

"You goddamned right I refuse," Fagin snarled.

"Even though I remind you that you are operating in our country?"

"Even then, Colonel Ngai," Fagin said. "And I resent your unkind and insulting remarks to Lieutenant Thuy."

Ngai, all pretense at politeness now gone, glared at Fagin. "I'll have you out of South Vietnam within the week!" He walked to the door and whirled to face Andrea. "And you, you alley cat, I'll have you shot!"

Fagin realized the man had become dangerously angry. "I think we should all reconsider what we've said here. It would be wise if—"

"I will reconsider nothing!" Ngai said in his high-pitched voice. Then he stepped from the office and left Fagin and Andrea standing in stunned silence.

The sound of the aircraft's engines was faint in the early night sky.

Archie Dobbs, staring upward, spoke to Sparks Jackson without looking. "How far out are they?"

"Five minutes," Sparks said, turning from his ever-faithful radio.

Archie and the entire detachment, except for Falconi and Sparks, had formed into a T formation. Each held his unlit flashlight pointing toward the sky.

Falconi judged the time to be right. "Okay, guys. Hit the lights."

The drop-zone marking effort, as simple as it was, did the job. The aircraft, a C-130, though invisible to them, grew louder as it lost altitude and lined up on the long stem of their T. It swooped down low along the proper line of flight.

Inside the fuselage, the crew chief nodded to the two doormen as the green lights in the bulkhead flashed on. Each of the pair kicked the door bundles out. They fell a short distance before the static lines jerked open the parachutes, rapidly and violently slowing the rate of descent.

The Black Eagles wasted little time in retrieving the cargo and lugging it from the open area of the drop zone into the darker area under the canopy of jungle trees.

The canvas covers were deftly opened, the contents passed out to the members of Top's Bravo team. New rucksacks, equipment, ammo, and rations were soon individually stowed by the men.

Robert Falconi sighed a bit with relief. Now the hunt for the unknown killers could really get serious.

CHAPTER SEVEN

Robert Mikhailovich Falconi was born in 1934 at Fort Meade, Maryland, near Washington, D.C.

His father, Second Lieutenant Michael Falconi, was a West Point graduate assigned to the Third Infantry Regiment at Fort Meade. His outfit was a largely ceremonial organization which performed such details as guarding the Tomb of the Unknown Soldier, conducting military funerals at Arlington National Cemetery, and providing the guard of honor for various official functions. During Lieutenant Falconi's bachelor days, his role in these capricious affairs was that of Protocol Officer.

These duties required that he be present during certain social events to see that everything was coordinated while the brass and political bigwigs had a good time. It was at one of these parties that he became acquainted with Miriam Ananova Silberman.

This most attractive young woman was a twenty-year-old member of the League of Jewish Refugees. A striking brunette with expressive eyes and a pleasant smile, Miriam Silberman had fled the anti-Semitic terror of Stalin's Russia with her father two years previously.

Her organization had been petitioning various members of the U.S. Congress for action in saving Jews not only from the Communist savagery but from the new threat of Hitler's Nazi Germany. These efforts had resulted in the young woman meeting certain high personages in the American government. These relationships with politicians deeply concerned over the peril faced by Europe's Jewry, resulted in Miriam Silberman's exposure to Washington social life. Eventually she received an invitation to attend a party that happened to be under the care and supervision of the protocol officer Michael Falconi.

When the young Lieutenant laid eyes on Miriam, he fell immediately in love. Later he would repeatedly say it was her eyes that cast the tenderest of spells on him. But whatever it was, he spent the rest of the evening hanging around her, ignoring his duties in his steadfast determination to get to know this enigmatic and beautiful Russian girl better. Not a dance went by that Lieutenant Falconi did not present himself to her. He constantly hovered nearby, making sure the young woman's punch glass was kept filled.

Miriam was fascinated by this unexpected attention. Michael Falconi was dark, handsome, and very charming. Before the evening was over, the infatuation had become mutual, and a serious courtship was begun by the earnest young officer.

Miriam's father, Josef Silberman, an elderly widower, was opposed to the match. He wanted her to marry a Jewish boy, but Miriam pointed out to him that America was most certainly not a homogeneous land and that the mixing of nationalities and religions in love was not all that unusual. The old man finally gave in to the young people's emotional ties and bestowed his blessings on the couple when they were married.

Their first and only child, Robert, was born a year later. His life, like theirs, was spent on various army posts. The only time he lived in a town was during the four years the father was serving in the European Theater of Operations. When Colonel Falconi returned stateside, the family resumed its nomadic army life going from post to post with each transfer.

Nonetheless, Robert Falconi had a happy childhood. Raised to speak English and Russian, he was fluent in both languages. During the several tours they spent in the Far East, the young boy became a serious and skillful practitioner of karate. He loved life, but had one problem: his complete, dedicated dislike of school.

The colonel wanted his son to follow in his footsteps and attend West Point. The nation's military academy had given him, the son of a poor Italian shoemaker, the chance for a fine education which had resulted in his acceptance as an officer and a gentleman in the army he truly loved.

Robert Falconi liked the army too. But in a slightly different way. He enlisted in 1951 after graduation from high school at age seventeen. Following basic and advanced infantry training he was sent to the fighting in Korea to serve in the Second Infantry Division. He came back a sergeant with a silver star, a purple heart, and the undying knowledge that he was a soldier through and through. And his martial ambitions had gone through a change too. Sergeant Falconi now wanted to be an officer like his father, but without gaining a commission in the demanding academia of the United States Military Academy. His maturation had not included any change in his attitude toward school books.

He reenlisted in the army and applied for Officers Candidate School at Fort Benning, Georgia.

The six months at the Infantry School were good ones for the young man. He excelled at everything — classroom work, field exercises, and even Fuck-Your-Buddy-Week where a man's conduct (or misconduct) was credited to another candidate. Falconi's "buddy" was late to a formation on one occasion and drew a gig during an inspection on another. It was Falconi who drew the demerits.

But despite these slight setbacks he came out on top of his class. His marks in efficiency and conduct were so superlative that he was offered a Regular Army commission. The young second lieutenant happily accepted the honor and settled in for a dedicated career in the army he had learned to love as much as his father did.

Falconi's first few years as an officer were spent in various schools. He went to jump school, ranger school, to the more mentally demanding infantry school at Fort Benning, Georgia, and then to the Command and General Staff School at Fort Leavenworth, Kansas, for advanced training. It was during this time that his intellectual side finally blossomed. He composed several articles for the *Infantry Journal,* expounding on theories and applications that had evolved from his military experience. After attending Jungle School in Panama, he wrote a series of pieces based on his analysis of the proper conduct of jungle and mountain operations involving insurgency and counterinsurgency measures.

Those last papers resulted in his return to Panama where he served on a special committee to develop official U.S. Army doctrine on combat in small groups under tropical conditions. His next duty assignment, following his volunteering for Special Forces, found him at Fort Bragg, North Carolina. Here he was once again immersed in training until his subsequent assignment to South Viet Nam during the early phases of that conflict.

Falconi served with the 5th Special Forces where he worked closely with ARVN troops and helped organize village militias for protection against VC attacks and pressure. His duties included organizing several dangerous missions which he also led. These operations involved deep penetration into enemy territory where the maximum destruction possible was inflicted on Communist forces.

Eventually he came into contact with Clayton Andrews, a CIA case officer assigned to Southeast Asia. Andrews, with his own operational requirements to meet, found the Special Forces officer a vigorous and enthusiastic participant during the times the intelligence agency required assistance from the Fifth. Finally, with the need for more and more clandestine missions, the necessity for a permanent unit of specialists in jungle, guerilla, and ranger-type operations became so pressing that a detachment was ordered formed under CIA supervision. This was done within the Special Operations Group which operated out of Peterson Field in Saigon.

Clayton Andrews, when put in charge of this project, didn't hesitate to call in Captain Robert Falconi, not only for advice and counsel, but to lead this new group that was to be known as the Black Eagles.

While their methods and planning were to be sophisticated and even exotic, the Black Eagles' real policy was to be simple and direct: *Kill or be killed*.

The men who were to be assigned to this special detachment were to be recruited from various branches of the military and were to include all nationalities involved in the struggle against the Communist encroachment into Southeast Asia. Thus, Americans, South Vietnamese, South Koreans, Australians, and others — soldiers, sailors, or airmen — were eligible for membership in this exclusive killing society. They were only required to possess the proper skills, determination, qualifications, and guts.

The Black Eagles wasted no time in getting into action following their official organization.

Their first mission was to hit a vacation retreat of Communist bigwigs in North Vietnam. Here the leaders of world socialism could relax and let down their hair as their every sexual whim and desire were catered to. Of course, this occurred far from the prying eyes of the slave populations who strove and sacrificed in the illegal struggle to force Marxism on people unwilling to accept its harsh tenants voluntarily.

The second operation involved a raid on a unique and elite prison camp run by the North Vietnamese. This facility, code-named Camp Three by the Reds, was designed to implement special interrogation techniques on prisoners who had propaganda or intelligence value. There was even a North Korean interrogation expert stationed at that POW camp. This cruel practitioner of torture and brainwashing had developed his skills on American pilots during the Korean War.

Falconi and his men not only ripped the place apart, they took all the prisoners, the North Koreans, and the camp commandant with them.

Clayton Andrews was promoted out of his job, and Chuck Fagin took his place as the Black Eagles' CIA case officer when a Russian attempt to establish a nuclear reactor in Laos caused the Black Eagles to undertake their third mission. The detachment went into this operation in a glider, silently infiltrating the dreaded Pathet Lao in a soaring night flight to destroy the plant and deal death to these ferocious followers of Marx.

Now their fourth mission, Operation Asian Blitzkrieg, was underway. They must find and destroy the unknown Caucasians who were posing as Americans while committing unspeakable atrocities. Chuck Fagin smelled a rat somewhere, but before he could set to work to seriously ferret out the danger, he found himself beset by Colonel Ngai Quang of the South Vietnamese Army who demanded full disclosure of the Black Eagles and their operations.

Fagin had no trust in Ngai despite his clearance by the American authorities. He knew the Communists were aware of the existence of a special detachment that was being used against them. And he knew they would want it destroyed as quickly as possible. Thus, giving out information on the Black Eagles was tantamount to signing a death sentence on each and every one of them. If they weren't compromised and massacred in combat, they would surely be assassinated the first time they surfaced in any part of Southeast Asia.

Fagin had been keeping the Black Eagles isolated in their base camp, denying them much-needed furloughs until he could sort things out. But Ngai's insistence and intrusions were making things more difficult and dangerous. Fagin was at the point where the old army cliché was certainly applicable:

Do something! Even if it's wrong, do something!

Fagin was going to do something. But for Falconi and the Black Eagles' sake, it had better be right.

Rolf Stahler sat in the thatch hut and reassembled the M-16 rifle he had just cleaned.

His men, all East German members of the *Bereitschaftpolizei,* were also tending to their gear. This special detachment, after many long days of tramping through the jungle, was taking a well-deserved rest.

They had pulled several raids on villages after shooting up the South Vietnamese army convoy. Even dedicated Communists needed time to refresh themselves and get away from work.

And they had to forget too.

No matter how cold-blooded a killing machine the state turned a man into, the act of shooting down scores of unarmed women and children took its psychological toll. Hitler's killer squads had found that out during routine massacres of Jews before the more sophisticated gas chambers were developed. The SS men assigned to the grim duties of murdering civilians numbed their feelings with liquor which was issued to them freely and generously by their superiors.

Stahler, while relatively unmoved himself, found that large quantities of Russian vodka kept his men on an even keel of sorts. He had seen to it that the Russian KGB colonel, Krashchenko, kept plenty coming their way in this miserable little camp they called home during the operation in Vietnam.

His thoughts were interrupted by the arrival of his second-in-command Leutnant Wilhelm Feldhaus. Feldhaus rapped on the doorway of the hut. *Kamerad Hauptmann?*"

"Yes, Willi?" Stahler responded.

"The local Viet Cong chief is here to see you. He says it's important."

"Send him in then," Stahler said. He was growing weary of the guerilla leader. The man seemed to think that European Communists had a direct link to the Kremlin. He was constantly hovering about offering advice and help while making a nuisance of himself.

A minute later, the black pajama-clad figure of Nguyen Han appeared at the door. "Ah, Comrade Nguyen. Please come in."

The VC stepped into the hut with two of his men. Each carried a pack of sorts. At a gesture from Nguyen they dropped the items to the floor and withdrew.

"What is this?" Stahler asked.

"We found these rucksacks washed up on the beach to the southeast of here," Nguyen explained. "Our examination makes us believe they belonged to Americans who may have lost them in the water."

Curious, Stahler knelt down and opened one of the still-damp packs. Inside he found a change of clothing, some C rations, cigarettes, and other items. The containers were sterile as far as identification was concerned. They had most definitely not been carried by regular troops. Stahler also took special note that the smokes had not deteriorated too much. They obviously hadn't spent much time in the water.

The East German stood up. "When were these found,

Comrade?"

"Early this morning, Comrade Captain."

"Did you search the immediate area?"

"As well as possible," Nguyen answered. "But we couldn't spend too much time on the open beach for fear of being discovered by the imperialists or their lackeys."

"Of course," Stahler said. He took the time to carefully check the contents of the second rucksack. "Has there been any unusual activity by the Americans in that particular territory?"

"No, Comrade Captain. None at all. In fact, neither myself nor my men have seen any sign of them in the vicinity," Nguyen answered. "That is why we thought it so curious that these things would be washed up. As you can see, they weren't in the water very long."

"Exactly," Stahler agreed. "Which means they were lost quite close to shore." He realized that if the Black Eagles were in the vicinity, they had enough skill in fieldcraft to avoid discovery for quite a long time. He thought for a moment. "Have there been any boat patrols?"

"None at all, Comrade Captain."

"Very well," Stahler said. "You did the correct thing in bringing these to me. Now I want you to increase reconnaissance patrols in that area. Also have your spies and auxiliaries be particularly alert. I think we may have unannounced visitors in our midst."

Nguyen nodded. "They want to surprise us."

Stahler smiled coldly. "That's what they wanted to do, no doubt. But now that we know they're in the area, we can be the ones arranging surprises — and they will be most unpleasant ones."

Nguyen grinned. "Yes, Comrade Captain. I will tend

to the matter now."

"On your way out, please send in Comrade Feldhaus," Stahler said. "We will have to step up the next phase of our own operation now."

CHAPTER EIGHT

Chun Kim, the Republic of Korea marine master sergeant, moved cautiously through the thick grove of trees. A scant one hour earlier he had volunteered to relieve the very fatigued Archie Dobbs as detachment scout.

Dobbs, who had performed on the point all the day before and during the previous night's traveling, had finally reached such a degree of exhaustion that even he had to admit he was tired.

Now, with Kim's grenade launcher across his weary shoulders, Archie enjoyed the relative leisure of moving along in the middle of the column rather than painstakingly breaking the trail and taking constant compass readings at the front. Falconi had even relieved him of having to maintain a security watch on one of the flanks.

Kim's offer to provide a break for the regular scout was not so much an act of kindness as an attempt to save face. During the Black Eagles' previous operation in Laos, Kim had collapsed under a very serious case of heatstroke. Any lesser man would have died from it.

And it wasn't his fault either. Newly arrived in South Vietnam, the Korean had been rushed out to the Special Forces B camp the Black Eagles called home. Then he had been committed to Operation Laos Nightmare without a chance to become acclimated to the heavy, humid heat of the area.

But to Kim this was no excuse.

Deep in his warrior's heart the Korean felt he had let his new comrades down, and he was more than ready to make up for what he considered an unbearable disgrace. He told none of the others of his determination to prove himself, but each and every Black Eagle sensed that Chun Kim was out to follow Dinky Dow's philosophy down to its basic tenant:

Kick ass!

And Kim couldn't think of a better place to do it than up at the head of the column which penetrated deeper into Viet Cong territory.

The jungle is an enigmatic and distracting environment in which to conduct war. Sometimes sound will carry virtually for miles, while at other times the natural arrangement of the vegetation might deaden noise to the extent that a man can't hear another on the opposite side of a narrow bamboo grove. Visibility, even during the brightest daylight hours, is always bad. The tight canopy of trees above the spongy, stinking ground blots out the sun until the densest parts of a rain forest may have the visual qualities of midnight — even at noon.

At night the blackness can be similar to that of a deep cave. Often, though a full, brilliant moon may hang high in the sky, the inkiness of the jungle makes it wiser for a man to cease all traveling and make no attempt to move in this opaque hell where booby traps and land mines may be waiting for the unwary.

Kim walked slowly, his booted feet making soft contact with the ground. He stopped now and turned to his compass to check his azimuth, but there was no real need to follow a strict route. The men now being sought by the Black Eagles could be anywhere within the Operational Area, and there were no trails to follow. There was only the clinging plant life, that had to be penetrated carefully and slowly with as little sound as possible.

The Korean marine eased through the thatch of palm fronds and suddenly found himself standing in a small clearing. He was as surprised as the VC who had made camp there. They hadn't even heard his approach.

Kim's M-16 muzzle came up and he squeezed the trigger. The first two rounds plowed into the head of the nearest Red guerrilla. The man, who had been stirring a pot of rice, was bowled over by the force of the bullets, blood and brains spraying from his shattered skull. He collided with another VC at his side. Kim swung the M-16 and put a quick shot into the belly of a third Red, then, continuing the action, stitched a fourth with two quick shots.

The second VC struggled out from under the body of his comrade and made a desperate dash for the woods. The Korean, slipping the selector switch over to full automatic, pulled back on the trigger and watched the bullets strike the fleeing man from the left thigh and up across his buttocks before dancing across his back leaving gaping, bloody wounds. The final slug slapped into the guerrilla's neck and exited his face taking nose, eyes, and brains out with it.

The entire episode had taken less than five seconds.

Falconi, with Dinky Dow and Archie on his heels, charged into the clearing and saw Kim standing calmly amidst the human carnage he had created.

Kim, his eyes creased almost shut because of his happy grin, threw a quick salute. "Big surprise for me, Skipper. Didn't expect VC so close."

Falconi nodded. "Big surprise for them, too, I'd say. From the looks of 'em, there's no survivors."

Dinky Dow quickly checked the bodies. "All dead, Falcon," he announced. "Look like a small patrol fucking off. Should have had security out."

"Yeah," Falconi agreed. "Sometimes Charlie can be the cleverest little bastard, and other times he can be the dumbest son of a bitch to walk the face of the earth."

Archie glanced at Kim. "Want me to take over now? I'm all rested up."

"I stay on point," Kim said. "Feel good. Want to kill more VC motherfucker, okay?"

"Sure," Falconi said grinning. "Carry on, Kim."

The Korean marine's grin increased in width for a second, then his face grew serious, and without hesitating, he stepped out of the clearing and went back to breaking the trail for the rest of the detachment.

"Are you outta your goddamned mind?"

Clayton Andrews stood in Chuck Fagin's office doorway and glared inside at his subordinate.

Fagin sighed and turned his attention away from his paper work. "I've been wondering how long it would be before you got here."

Andrews strode into the room and put his hands on the desk, leaning toward Fagin. "You insulted one of South Korea's top intelligence officials, Chuck! And he's damned mad about it."

"Piss on Ngai," Fagin said.

"It's *you* that's gonna get pissed on, buddy!" Andrews said. "Ngai is so mad he can't see straight. He's been right to the American ambassador, and he's howling so loud they'll soon hear him in Washington."

"I don't trust the sonofabitch, Andy," Fagin said. "And there wasn't any directive from my own people that I cooperate with him. All he had was a request from the South Vietnamese government."

Andrew's eyes rolled toward the ceiling in anger. "That's *all* he had, huh? Just a goddamned request from the goddamned South Vietnamese government, that's all, huh?"

"Sure," Fagin said defensively. "I'm not required to follow any direct orders — or requests — from them."

"Of course not," Andrews said. "But that doesn't give you the right to tell the guy to go shit in his hat."

"I didn't say that to him," Fagin said defensively.

"You might as well have," Andrews fumed. "Why the hell didn't you just grab him and bang his fucking head against the wall? It would have gotten the same results. You made the guy lose face, Chuck. And in front of a countrywoman too."

"Andrea doesn't like him any better than I do," Fagin said.

"That makes it worse," Andrews said. He calmed down and took a seat in the dilapidated chair in front of the desk. "You're gonna make up for this, you know that?"

"I don't know shit."

"You're gonna write a goddamned letter of apology, Chuck — and address it directly to Colonel Ngai Quang.

In that same letter you're gonna invite his scrawny ass over here to give him the information he wants."

Fagin leaned back in his chair and composed the missive aloud. "Let's see . . . Dear Colonel Ngai, I'm sorry I talked bad to you. Get your scrawny ass over here and I'll tell you all about the fucking Black Eagles. Your pal, Chuck . . . " He scowled at Andrews. "How's that?"

"Don't be a wiseass," Andrews said. "I want a good letter, and a thorough briefing on Falconi and his men prepared for Ngai."

"I don't trust the son-of-a-bitch, goddamnit!" Fagin exclaimed.

"Jesus Christ! He's been cleared by the Agency," Andrews said. "Ngai even attends intelligence briefings at MAC V. But that's not good enough for you, is it?"

"No way," Fagin insisted.

"Okay, Chuck, okay," Andrews relented. "You tell me what you got on the guy, and if it's good enough, I'll go as far as I can to neutralize him."

"I don't have anything on him," Fagin said. "It's instinct, Andy. Pure blind gut feeling that tells me the son-of-a-bitch is up to no good. And that goes back to my OSS days in Yugoslavia."

Andrews shook his head. "You expect me to trot back to the upper echelons and tell them to put a damper on Colonel Ngai Quang because Chuck Fagin *supposes* he's a risk in some obscure, mysterious way."

"Sure."

Andrews stared at Fagin for one incredulous moment, then stood up. "Write the fucking letter, prepare the fucking report, then get back to me. I want to hear that's all been accomplished within forty-eight hours."

Fagin hung his head and spoke softly. "Okay . . . goddamn it to hell . . . okay!"

Andrews went to the door. "You really fucked up, Chuck. I stuck my neck out for you, but I can't do much if you go around insulting the ARVN brass."

"Fuck the ARVN brass," Fagin said. "I don't want Falconi and his guys knocked off through some filthy double cross."

"Do as you're told," Andrews said. He stepped through the door and slammed it shut.

Fagin sat for a long time, then pulled a sheet of paper from his desk to begin the first draft of the letter of apology to Ngai. After that he would prepare the report that would bare the hearts and souls of the Black Eagles.

The ambush exploded from Kim's right rear.

He whirled in that direction and blasted out with a fusillade of semiautomatic firing before charging in the direction of the attack.

The other Black Eagles, responding per the Detachment SOP, also cut loose with volleys toward the origin of the assault and rushed the enemy positions. The success of these first shots was evidenced by three dead Charlies—one had his entire lower jaw blown away to leave a gaping, red cavern below his mutilated nose—sprawled in the brush.

But there were others dug in better a bit farther back into the jungle. They had chosen their positions carefully and, with good fields of fire, they suddenly raked the Black Eagles.

The big Australian, Tommy Newcomb, spun under the impact of a round that hit his shoulder. Dizzy and surprised, he tried to move back out of range but a second shot crashed into his right buttock. That leg gave out and he fell clumsily to the ground. Rapidly going into shock, he was struggling back to his feet when the third and final bullet from the Russian Kalashnikov AK-47 assault riffle zapped into the SAS man's skull, blowing out all consciousness and life-sustaining functions.

Meanwhile, Kim on the left flank of the battle had correctly doped out the situation. The Viet Cong had drawn the Black Eagles into a cleverly laid ambuscade in which a few ineffectives had been sacrificed in order to pull them in closer. Now the better enemy soldiers had a clear view of them.

The Korean, using the distinctive sound of the AK-47s to locate the main enemy line, continued unobserved past them until he reached a point where he could turn back and come up behind the Charlies.

Kim moved swiftly now, the sound of the fighting building up and covering the noise of his impromptu infiltration of the Red's positions. He found the first one squatting behind the thick trunk of a tree. The Korean, a third dan black belt in *Tae-kwon-do* Korean karate, moved up to the rear of the guerrilla. He hissed a silent *kiah* to avoid alerting the enemy and lashed an *ahp-bahl-keum-chi* stroke to the man's right kidney. The powerful ball-of-the-foot kick ruptured the tender organ. The Ho Chi Min flunky convulsed in agony. But his pain was brief as the ROK marine swiftly moved in and locked a lightning-quick-forearm-vise hold on the unfortunate VC.

Kim applied increased leverage and savagely twisted his shoulders. The man's neck snapped like a lead pencil. The shooting had grown in intensity now, making the Korean marine hurry. Shots sounding above his head gave away the position of a tree sniper. Kim looked upward. It took him several moments to locate the man, but finally he could make out the VC's figure high in the tree. The Korean took carefully aim, waited for a fusillade to sound from the other Viet Cong positions to cover the sound of his own shots, then cut loose with a round from his M-16.

The bullet smacked the Charlie in the right foot and continued through to smash through his penis and lodge in the guerrilla's lower bowels. Badly hurt, but still physically capable, the Viet Cong instinctively returned fire in the direction from which he had been attacked.

Kim didn't blink an eye. He traded shot for shot with the injured man until he scored a hit. The Red slipped off the bough he'd been standing on and crashed through the limbs to hit the ground at the Korean's feet.

There were two more enemy positions to go. Since they might inflict heavy casualties on the Black Eagles, Kim decided to use his hand grenades. He tossed the explosive devices at the sound of two more Kalashnikovs and was rewarded with a sudden silence.

Unexpectedly fresh shots exploded, but the Korean realized these were from the Black Eagles.

"Hey!" he shouted. "It me Kim! No more shoot. All VC motherfucker dead now."

A minute later Falconi, Dinky Dow, and Top Gordon appeared through the brush. The team sergeant slapped Kim on the shoulder. "It's a damn good thing you got back here. We couldn't figure out where these bastards were."

"Right," Falconi agreed. "If we'd withdrawn, they'd have just come out after us."

Kim, finally pleased that he had demonstrated some

value to his comrades, let his face fold back into an enthusiastic grin. "Ever'body, okie-dokie, Skipper?"

"I'm afraid not," Falconi said. "Newcomb bought the farm."

"Yeah," Top enjoined. "Caught several rounds at the start of the fire fight."

Kim felt genuinely saddened by the news. He and the big Australian had begun to grow close, forming a friendship that had shown the potential for blossoming into a deeper relationship — the kind that can only be fostered between men who face danger together.

Kim, as emotional as any of his countrymen, made no attempt to stem the flow of tears that welled in his eyes. "We call in chopper for Tommy, Skipper?"

"I'm afraid we can't," Falconi said. "Too much of a chance it'd compromise whatever security we may have. We'll have to bury him here. Don't worry, Kim. I'll make note of the grid coordinates of his grave and have Sparks radio them in. Eventually there'll be a body recovery detail sent out for him. Okay?"

"Okay. Then I take care of him, Skipper," Kim said pulling his entrenching tool from its carrier on his pistol belt. "He my friend. I put Tommy away."

The four men walked back to where the detachment had set up a hasty defensive perimeter. Staff Sergeant Tom Newcomb, Australian Special Air Service, lay in the middle, his bullet-torn body sprawled under his poncho.

Archie Dobbs, standing beside Falconi, wiped at the sweat streaking through his dirty face. "Damn, Skipper, I hope this fucking operation doesn't turn into another bloody deal like Operation Song Bo Slaughter. We got away without casualties on the last mission. Our luck may have run out this trip."

"I hate to say it, Archie," Falconi said glancing down at Tommy's covered cadaver, "but it looks like you could be right. This is developing into a real hairy situation."

CHAPTER NINE

The line of prisoners moved forward with the stoic endurance and patience that only Orientals can display.

Each of the dozen men had his hands bound tightly behind him. And all were connected by a single rope in which loops had been fashioned to fit around their necks. If one fell, he would drag all his fellow sufferers down with him — painfully to choke until their guards relieved the pressure of the crude nooses.

Rolf Stahler sweating profusely in the heavy humidity of the close jungle, held up his hand to signal a halt. His assistant, Kamerad Leutnant Willi Feldhaus hurried forward from the center of the column which had been traveling since early dawn. The young officer, wearing American jungle fatigues like the rest of the East Germans guarding the prisoners, saluted.

Stahler took off his helmet and ran his hands through his sweat-soaked hair. "We are near the vicinity of the yesterday's battle, Willi."

"*Jawohl, Kamerad Hauptmann,*" Feldhaus said. "It is a great shame that Nguyen's men didn't wipe out the Yankee swine or at least take some prisoners."

"They did manage to kill one of them," Stahler remarked. "There was a lot of blood soaked into the ground in that one location. And their footprints made it appear they were one man less."

"Being able to read tracks is a great asset, *Kamerad Hauptmann*," Willi said.

"When we return to East Germany I will see to it that you receive a billet in the *Grenzpolizei* school," Stahler said. "The Frontier Police can make you an expert at that particular craft in the matter of only a few weeks."

"Thank you, *Kamerad Hauptmann*," Feldhaus said.

"Well, let's begin baiting our traps, Willi," Stahler said. "Bring out three of the prisoners."

The young officer turned and issued quick orders. A pair of the East Germans separated three of their captives from the line of other prisoners and shoved them forward to a point in front of their commander.

Stahler lit a cigarette, then pulled the American .45 automatic pistol from the holster. He raised the weapon into the face of the nearest prisoner and pulled the trigger.

The man's facial bones folded in from the impact of the large slug. Almost simultaneously the back of his head exploded outward with the bullet's exit.

Without hesitation, Stahler swung the pistol to the next prisoner and repeated the procedure. One more shot and all three bodies, their hands still bound, lay at his feet. *"Sehr gut!"* he said. "Let's move out to the next point."

Still not registering any emotion, the remaining nine captives walked past their dead friends as the East Germans pushed them along the route they wished to them to follow.

"We'll lead the imperialists straight into our arms with this bait," Feldhaus said.

"I only hope it isn't too obvious," Stahler said.

"Are you sure these men are the men we're after, *Kamerad Hauptmann?*"

"We haven't had any firm confirmation as of yet, but I would say from all indications that those rucksacks Nguyen's men found belonged to the *Schwarzenadler* — the Black Eagles."

"I wonder how long it will be before that Russian *Schweinhund* Krashchenko can let us know," Feldhaus remarked angrily. "I don't trust those bastards."

Stahler laughed. "What intelligent German — East or West — does?"

"Those bastards are going to get theirs someday, believe me," Feldhaus said.

"Shhh!" Stahler cautioned him. "There is probably a trusted KGB man among our small troop here. You wouldn't want to be reported for rebellious remarks made about the Soviet Union, would you?"

Feldhaus shrugged. "We'll have those *scheistköpfe* off our backs some day, then we can speak of them as we like."

"Of course," Stahler said bitterly. "And both parts of our country will be joined together soon too, *nicht wahr?*"

"I'll be patient," Feldhaus said.

"Here's a good spot," Stahler said, again calling a halt. "If the Yankees are searching around after finding the first three, they'll surely come this way. Get two this time. And you take care of them, Willi."

"Jawohl, Kamerad Hauptmann."

The young officer went back and detached the front

two Vietnamese from the remaining seven. He kicked and pummeled them forward. Without hesitating he held his M-16 rifle cradled in his arm and pulled the trigger.

The first man leaped back from the force of the bullet's entry and fell dragging his friend down with him. The survivor, his lips trembling in fear, grimaced as he waited for the final seal to be placed on his fate.

"You left them hooked together, Willi," Stahler said, laughing.

Feldhaus, embarrassed, angrily dispatched the second of the duo with two quick shots to the head. "Sorry, *Kamerad Hauptmann.*"

The small column moved out again. After twenty more minutes of slow travel, they again halted. This time three of the Vietnamese were shot. This trio was also left, hands tied, in a bloody pile.

The last four Vietnamese meekly allowed themselves to be pushed along. Each man already considered himself dead. As far as they were concerned their karma— that undeniable, uncontrollable fate that controls each person's destiny—had ordained that this be the day they died. If it hadn't been for the big Americans who had come to their village and taken them away to shoot them, then a tiger would have gotten them—or a cobra— or some accident would have befallen them. They could only accept their hard luck and hope that the next life would be better.

The small column was halted and there was no hesitation in the shooting of the four villagers. Within a few short moments their bodies, still twitching, lay amidst the blood-splattered ferns on the soft jungle floor.

Stahler turned to Feldhaus. "Our bait is laid. All we

can do now is to see if the prey takes it. But I want to emphasize one thing. Comrade Colonel Krashchenko wants the leader of these °Americans taken alive. He is part Russian and is subject to Soviet law. The KGB has great plans for him."

"He is the one named Falconi, *nicht wahr?*"

"The same," Stahler answered.

"Then I think we ought to shoot the *Schwein,*" Willi Feldhaus said. "Even his being part Russian is enough for me to want to destroy him."

Stahler laughed. "There is something else you should know about Falconi. I understand he is also part Jewish."

"*Jude!*" Feldhaus spat. "Now I know I'll want to kill him, *Kamerad Hauptmann!*"

"Control yourself, Willi," Stahler said soothingly. "Remember the KGB is watching us."

Colonel Ngai Quang of the Army of the Republic of Vietnam, lived in a large house in one of the richest neighborhoods of Saigon. This area, inhabited by big-wigs of the armed forces and government — along with many foreign VIP's — was an armed camp unto itself. Special guard units patrolled the streets and manned the entrances into this hallowed sanctuary of the local elite.

Ngai was the son of a wealthy businessman. He had done the unspeakable as a young man, however, by refusing to follow the career chosen for him by his parents. Ngai loved uniforms and pomp, and had opted for the military as a profession. But since he was extremely small and thin even for a Vietnamese, he had found the rigors of life in combat a bit too much to bear. So he had ended up on staff details — eventually settling for the intelligence section. He still got to wear a fancy uniform with epaulettes and all the trimmings. Besides, Ngai really wasn't that crazy about lugging a pack through the jungle as an infantry officer.

And promotion was slower there anyway.

Ngai did make one concession to his parents. He agreed to marry the rather homely daughter of one of the family's business associates. This aided his father in forming a commerical alliance of sorts and put Ngai back into good standing at home. He endured his wife by ignoring her as much as possible. She didn't seem to mind a bit; actually, her own feelings for Ngai bordered on loathing.

But between his army position and a generous allowance from both his own family and his wife's, Ngai enjoyed the better things of Vietnamese society. Fancy cars, expensive clothing, jewelry, and the best of American and Japanese appliances filled his life.

As did his favorite pastime — gambling.

Westerners who become addicted to gambling are in a bad way. For the Oriental it is a hell on earth. The roll of the dice, turn of the card, or as in Ngai's favorite game, the draw of the mah-jongg tile is more addictive than a narcotic.

Ngai loved to go to the Chinese section of Saigon. There he would spend entire nights in an orgy of gaming. He made reckless, insane bets as he lost a small fortune over a relatively short period of time. This activity brought him to the attention of certain Communist agents and operatives who had been placed and financed into the gambling trades by their superiors in Hanoi, Peking, and even Moscow.

They concentrated on finding people like Ngai — big

shots in sensitive positions who had no control over their gaming instincts. It didn't take them long to "make" Ngai and to put the army officer into an insidious program designed to suck him into their power.

In the beginning of the carefully manipulated scheme, he won huge amounts of money. His luck was phenomenal as each night he raked in his winnings at the mah-jongg tables of an establishment known as Tsing Chai's. After a while his luck diminished slightly, but only for a short time. It rallied and he was soon winning big again.

Another bit of backsliding was changed with a quick recovery, then suddenly the bottom fell out. He could do nothing right. Within a few months he had amassed an extremely large debt to Tsing Chai himself—the owner of Ngai's favorite mah-jongg parlor.

Finally the situation was impossible. Ngai owed so much, that he faced absolute ruin in both his personal and professional life.

Tsing Chai, an obscenely obese man, was well known in the vice and criminal circles of Saigon. But none of his contacts, among his fellow gangsters or the police, was aware the fat Chinese was a cleverly placed agent of the Communists. When Ngai had gotten in so deep that the time was right to approach him, Tsing Chai didn't waste a moment.

It was just before dawn. Ngai, red-eyed and fatigued after a long night's work at the table, stood up dejectedly. His head was bowed in despair and resignation to his terrible situation. He was completely and totally in financial ruin.

Tsing, seeing his chance from across the room, padded over to the Vietnamese army officer in his soft slippers. "My dear *Dai Ta* Nagi," the gambling boss said. "I am so sorry to hear of your long run of bad luck."

"Nor am I overjoyed with the misfortune," Ngai replied. "It appears that I owe you much money. And, I am sorry to say, more than I can repay within a reasonable period of time."

"Let us go into my office and see what can be done about this most dreadful and unbearable situation," Tsing Chai said. "I think there is a way you may be able to ease your indebtedness to my humble parlor."

Ngai, despite his secret misgivings, followed the Chinese back to his private rooms. There, the colonel learned that Tsing Chai required a list of names—a harmless roster of the recent graduates of the South Vietnamese Army's school for intelligence officers.

The debt was reduced and credit extended. Thus Ngai continued gambling—and giving in to Tsing Chai's demands. Soon he found himself turning over top-secret papers until he became so compromised there was no way out except court-martial or suicide.

Ngai had been caught in the classical trap. To turn in Tsing Chai and his cohorts way to expose himself too. There was absolutely no safe or honorable was to escape the situation.

The colonel decided that he would get what he could out of life; thus he continued gambling while, in effect, he became a bona-fide Communist agent, feeding Tsing Chai whatever intelligence he demanded.

Ngai received money—which he gambled away—and certain presents—which he couldn't. The latter were not given to him out of generosity or even appreciation. If he had been allowed to accrue many debts, Ngai would eventually come under the eyes of South

Vietnamese counter-intelligence. Then his secret existence — and Tsing Chai — would be discovered. But since he had a nice house, an automobile, and other luxuries, no one would suspect Ngai of ever being entrapped by gambling into throwing away large sums of money. The outward life he led seemed to be that of a respectable, patriotic army officer from the upper classes.

His latest assignment has been to set forward motions within the hierarchy of ARVN intelligence to gain access to all information regarding SOG's Black Eagle Detachment — and he was to make sure he was the officer appointed to receive the data.

From all appearances, Colonel Ngai was about to fulfill those requirements to a T.

Archie Dobbs looked up from the corpses. "This is the second batch, Skipper."

Falconi stared down at the dead men. Already fly-covered and smelling, their bloated flesh bit into the bonds that held their dead hands tied together. "I really want to get my mitts on those sons of bitches."

"I haven't seen anything like that since Korea," Top Gordon said. "I remember the first few months when the North Koreans were executing our guys in bunches."

"I've killed men before," Falconi said. "But I'll be damned if I could take some innocent guy and just blow him away. It takes a certain mentality I guess."

"Want to press on, Skipper?" Archie asked.

"Yeah. It looks like we're hot on their trail," Falconi answered. "And I'm looking forward to a showdown with the bastards."

Top Gordon nodded. "From all appearances I'd say

we're most certainly headed in the right direction."

Dinky Dow spoke impatiently from where he stood in column. "Let's go. Kick ass, eh?"

Falconi took a last look at the cadavers. "I can tell you for sure that somebody's ass is going to be kicked before this thing's over."

"It's going to be a real bad situation if we don't put a stop to this," Top added as he once again surveyed the pitiful sight of the men who had been so cold-bloodedly murdered. "The longer it goes on, the more folks in Southeast Asia are going to be convinced that it's GI's doing it."

"Well," Falconi said with a deep breath. "Standing around here and feeling sorry for these poor, dead people isn't going to get the job done." He nodded to Archie Dobbs. "Lead on, my friend. We'll go where you and destiny lead us."

"Real dramatic, Skipper," Archie said. "I hope neither one of us fucks you up."

CHAPTER TEN

The East German soldier lay concealed in the foliage. He peered carefully out of his cover at the jungle around him.

The observation post he occupied had been personally chosen by Kamerad Hauptmann Stahler. It was the most advanced and, consequently, the most dangerous. Despite this, the soldier considered it an honor to have been picked for the perilous assignment. It showed his commander had confidence in him.

This particular East German Communist zealot had proven himself a capable and effective member of the *Bereitschaftpolizei* not only in the slaughter of the miserable Vietnamese peasants, but back home during operations against his fellow countrymen too. He was a cold-blooded automaton who obeyed the orders of his superiors with effectiveness though without too much imagination or ingenuity.

But he was developing individualistic skills in jungle fighting now. Certain aspects of operating in this hostile and unfamiliar environment had begun to occur to him.

Unfortunately for the young Red, however, this growing expertise didn't increase fast enough or soon enough to save his life.

Archie Dobbs's muscular arm slid around his neck and clamped down hard.

As the blood flow to the brain was sharply curtailed, the American slapped his hand tightly over the German's mouth and nose to stifle any outcries. Within moments the kid went limp. Archie slowly and cautiously lowered the body to the ground. Then he drew his boot knife and sliced deeply into the jugular vein. Blood gushed out with each beat of the soldier's Marxist heart. When Archie was satisfied that there would be no recovery, he moved back toward the Black Eagles.

Fifteen minutes later he was squatting close to Falconi, Master Sergeant Top Gordon, and Lieutenant Dinky Dow.

"How'd it look out there, Archie?" Falconi whispered.

"There'r about twenty Caucasians—make that nineteen—over there, Skipper," Archie explained in a low voice.

"That's only about half the number that ARVN officer reported," Falconi mused. "He said it looked like two platoons that massacred his convoy."

"The other half must be back as a reserve or resting up," Top supposed.

"At any rate, they're spread out as skirmishers about eighty yards," Archie continued. He indicated the exact location on the map that sat on the ground between the four of them. "From the way they're lookin' off into the bush, they don't know for sure where we are. But they seem damn sure about what direction we're comin' from."

Falconi nodded. "Yeah. Their commander is probably planning on us hitting some portion of their positions, then they'll fold in and surround us."

"Fuck 'em," Archie hissed.

"Yeah," Dinky Dow said. "Kick ass!"

Falconi studied the map for a few moments; then he made up his mind what he would do. "There's no particular advantage in taking the time to get behind 'em. So we'll have the Alpha Team make first contact right in the middle of their line. Then we'll turn toward the right and meet their attack from that direction. After we settle with them we can take care of the rest."

"I see what you have in mind, Skipper," Top said. "With all of us pushing off in one direction their opposite flank won't be able to make contact until we turn and hit 'em."

"Right. And that'll be on our own terms when we're ready," Falconi said. "And remind your guys that we want prisoners."

"Gonna be tough," Dinky Dow said, "Everybody pissed off because Tommy dead."

"Yeah," Falconi agreed. "If you see any of your guys about to do in one of the baddies that could be captured, make him stop. We want healthy POWS if we can get 'em. It'd be tough to lug a couple of wounded with us. It's a ways back to where any decent LZ can be established." He turned to Archie. "What'd you think of what you saw?"

"Like I said, they're Caucasians. And a bunch of tough-looking dudes too," Archie answered. "But it's easy to tell they're not used to this area yet. They seem to be pretty tired and uncomfortable."

"I'm curious as hell about their nationality," Top said.

"Did you hear any of 'em talk?"

"Only from a distance. They're damn well disciplined and didn't make any noise. Even if I didn't catch any words I could tell the accent wasn't American."

"We'll soon know who the assholes are," Falconi said. "Let's get the boys ready to move out."

Stahler spoke urgently into the American Prick-6 radio for the sixth time. He glanced over at Leutnant Feldhaus. "The kid at the advanced observation post doesn't answer."

"Maybe he fell asleep," Feldhaus said angrily. "He can be shot for that."

"I doubt it," Stahler said. "As tired as these men are, they're hand-picked and eager. Especially that one. You'd better go check him out. And be careful."

"*Jawohl, Kamerad Hauptmann,*" Feldhaus said. He had been laying down with his weapon ready, facing the direction they expected the *Schwarzenadler* to come from. He got to his feet and moved forward to find the observation post. The lieutenant was irritated. If that *dummkopf* kid had dozed off he'd shoot him on the spot.

After traveling forward some fifty meters, Feldhaus pulled aside a large palm frond and stepped into the OP area. The young soldier was lying down alright, but it didn't take the *Kamerad Leutnant* more than a cursory glance at the pool of blood around the kid's head to figure out he wasn't napping. A slight movement in the brush in front of him caused Feldhaus to look up.

Popeye Jenkins's ancient face appeared. The UDT man wasted no time in getting off a quick shot at the East German in the American uniform.

The M-16's bullet punched through Feldhaus's hel-

114

met and zipped around the interior to drop out in front of him. Meantime, he had instinctively pulled a grenade loose from his patrol harness and flung it at the American.

Then he turned and fled.

The explosive bounced between Popeye's legs and rolled a scant two feet before going off. The shrapnel hit the sailor, but it had been deflected and slowed by the thick vegetation. Nonetheless, the concussion still had enough force to knock him, face down, into the stinking jungle earth.

"You no good son-of-a-bitch!" Popeye screamed in rage. "You just fucked with the wrong guy!"

He fired wildly in the direction of the fleeing German before he scrambled back deeper into the natural cover afforded by the rain forest.

Some hundred meters behind Stahler and his men, Nguyen Han, the Viet Cong guerrilla chief, had heard the shot followed almost instantly by the explosion of a grenade. He turned to his assistant and grinned widely, displaying his large, yellow teeth.

"Ah! The gangsters have made contact with the European comrades. We will soon have our orders to join the battle." He switched on his radio as per instructions and stuck the instrument to his ear in readiness to receive orders.

The other VC gripped his AK-47 tighter. "No doubt the imperialists are not expecting us to be in the vicinity."

Stahler had already issued his preliminary orders before the battle had actually commenced. His force was instructed to act quickly once the fighting began. Any men who were assaulted straight-on would counterattack in that same direction. The others would begin an enveloping sweep until they were in contact with the *Schwarzenadler*. With luck, they would have the swine surrounded and beaten into submission without having to rely on their Viet Cong comrades for help.

He would much rather have had the other half of his East German detachment with him, but he had been forced to rotate the men's field activities until they got more used to operating in the wet heat of Vietnam. Thus, he had to rely on Nguyen's VC band for support.

When Feldhaus rushed back he reported his encounter breathlessly. "The soldier at the observation post has been killed. And I saw one of the *Schwarzenadler!* It was an elderly man with a pinched face, *Kamerad Hauptmann. Mein Got im Himmel!* He was horrible looking! I threw a grenade at the old bastard," he said. He removed his helmet and stuck a finger through the hole in it. "See where he shot me?" Feldhaus's forehead was scratched where the bullet had scraped his skin during the time it had whipped around the interior of his heavy headgear.

"You're lucky to be alive," Stahler marveled. "But was he really old? I can't imagine the Americans sending their version of the *Volksheer* over here to Southeast Asia."

"Believe me, *Kamerad Hauptmann,*" Feldhaus said sincerely. "He was *alt und hasslich* — old and ugly! I think the Americans must use him to frighten their enemies."

"It sounds like he was wearing a mask," Stahler mused.

"Ach, nein, mein Kamerad Hauptmann! It was his own face," Feldhaus insisted.

Falconi listened intently as Dinky Dow's Alpha Team took the initial brunt of the fighting. With Tommy Newcomb dead, the grenadier's chores had fallen to Horny Galchaser. The sounds of bursting 40-millimeter ammunition showed that the Cherokee Indian was keeping his friends well supported in the density of the jungle.

Within five minutes of first contact, the Black Eagles received fire on both flanks. This was what Falconi had been waiting for. He hit the transmit button on his Prick-Six radio and spoke tersely.

"Execute! Execute!"

Simultaneously, the Alpha Team pulled back to break off fighting with the enemy's front positions. They turned toward the right flank at the same time Top Gordon's Bravos charged in that direction.

Lightfingers O'Quinn and Calvin Culpepper, side by side, burst through the thick vegetation and spotted two men wearing olive-drab American jungle fatigues. Without hesitation, both Black Eagles pumped 5.56-millimeter rounds in that direction.

The East Germans, not expecting to hit the *Schwarzenadler* for another couple of minutes, screamed in surprise and pain as bullets flew into them like buzzing steel hornets. They jerked and staggered in uncoordinated dances of death before flopping over to the ground.

The two Black Eagles, with Kim behind them, leaped over the bodies and continued their rapid advance.

Up to the right, Malpractice McCorckel and Top Gordon found targets. The medic, acting as the team's automatic rifleman, fired several firebursts of four and five rounds into a tightly grouped trio of these strangers

117

dressed as Americans. Top's steady semi-auto shots added accuracy to the volume and all three were knocked rolling to the dirt by the volley. The Black Eagles had faced eight of the East Germans on that right flank. With five of them now down, the survivors made an instinctive withdrawal.

Falconi knew it was time to change directions and slam into the other group of unsuspecting strangers. Again he gave his commands in the simplest terms as he spoke into the small radio.

"Reverse! Reverse!"

Horny Galchaser, who had just fired a grenade from his launcher, stopped in midstride. He broke his weapon open for reloading.

The bullet that hit him was a wild one. It had been fired only for effect by an East German out of sight in the thick brush.

The slug went into Horny's right arm pit, hit the scapula, then continued into his heart. He died instantly, collapsing onto his back with the M-79, still waiting to be loaded, laying across his stomach. None of his friends knew he had been hit.

Everyone else was too busy reversing the direction of the attack in order to swing back and hit the unsuspecting enemy who had counted on finding them much sooner. Thrown off balance, the Reds had stopped. The coordinated assault of the Black Eagles hit them hard. Volleys of M-16 bullets swept through them, downing four before the remaining five broke and fled.

Stahler was confused.

He could hear the fighting moving off to his left. He had expected a battle royal in the exact center of the combat area. But somehow his right flank had failed to make contact. Then suddenly the fighting stopped for a couple of beats. Now firing again erupted. This time over to his right. The realization of what had happened dawned on him immediately.

The Black Eagle commander, expecting to be hit on all sides, had concentrated his men in an assault on one area. When that had been dealt with, he reversed his direction and struck back at the other flank which was confused and puzzled by then.

There was no time to waste.

He alerted Nguyen and his VC to move in and lend a hand.

Falconi and the others maintained their pressure, but it was difficult to keep the fighting at a high intensity with the enemy seemingly doing their best to avoid contact.

Top Gordon concentrated hard on keeping his men aligned and operating in a fire-and-maneuver scheme. The problem was that the density of the vegetation and the fluid flow of fighting made any coordinated effort all but impossible.

Calvin Culpepper, who had been working closely with Lightfingers, suddenly found himself alone. He continued to move forward, covering himself with frequent bursts of fire to his front while listening for commands from Top, Falconi, or even Dinky Dow over in Alpha Team.

Luckily for Calvin he spotted the VC before the Red saw him. The black demo man made an accurate snap shot that slapped into the Viet Cong's chest. But others suddenly appeared and their combined fire caused

Calvin to make an undignified withdrawal. Soon the intensity of the shooting forced him to break into a run.

He continued fleeing while angling off into the direction where his teammates should be. He leaped through a low palm bush and came out the other side. The vegetation increased in density and he crashed through it like a powerful running back piling through persistent linebackers.

Then he stumbled over the body and struck the ground face down.

Calvin rolled over on his back and looked at Jack Galchaser's dead countenance. Horny's expression was calm, almost serene, as he lay on his back in the thick jungle grass.

Calvin emitted a cry of anguish. He struggled to his feet and started to examine his friend. He had only enough time to determine that Horny was dead before the yelling approach of the Viet Cong caused him to turn and renew his flight for safety.

CHAPTER ELEVEN

Lieutenant Colonel Gregori Krashchenko took the written version of the recently arrived radio message and read the few words scrawled there.

Despite its briefness, the contents were enough to make him smile. He laid it down on his desk and walked up to the blackboard mounted on the wall of his office. Across the top, written in English, were the words:

ROSTER OF THE
BLACK EAGLES DETACHMENT

He picked up the eraser and rubbed out one of the names. Across from him, seated at his own desk, Major Truong Van watched the Russian's activities with interest. "Has one of that gang of bandits been killed, Comrade Colonel?

Krashchenko smiled. "Yes. The message center just brought me a communiqué from Stahler. They've had their first encounter with Major Falconi's men and have managed to kill the one called Jack Galchaser. They even have his body in their possession. They will forward a photograph of the cadaver at the first opportunity."

He left the blackboard and handed the slip of paper to the North Vietnamese.

"It would appear our latest plan is working then," Truong remarked with a smile.

"Most assuredly, Comrade Major," Krashchenko said returning to his desk

The Russian, an officer of the KGB, had been assigned to Hanoi primarily as an observer and reporter on American military activities in Southeast Asia. When the existence of the supersecret Black Eagles Detachment was finally uncovered through the efforts of agents and the ARVN turncoat Ngai, the Soviets had charged Krashchenko with the job of directing all efforts to destroy the unit and capture its commander.

The latter requirement for the apprehension of the Black Eagle leader was considered all important by the Communist intelligence chiefs.

Major Falconi, with a Russian mother, could legally be considered a Russian citizen under their law. If he could be taken as a prisoner, his intelligence and propaganda value would be beyond estimation. A public trial as a war criminal—after a thorough wringing out through the KGB's efficient interrogation system—would yield countless benefits to the proponents of World Communism.

The supersecret outfit had finally come to Krashchenko's attention after the raid on the Camp Three prison in the north near Dien Bien Phu. A full disclosure of the unit's name and the men assigned to it had finally arrived through the spy network supervised by the wily Chinese agent Tsing Chai. With the ARVN turncoat Ngai Quang applying more and more pressure on the Americans, it wouldn't be too much longer before Krashchenko would know the Black Eagles' operations plans at about the same time that Major Falconi was informed of them.

Major Truong Van had been assigned as an aide to the Russian as well as the official representative of North Vietnam's military intelligence. He aided his Soviet counterpart in coordinating Hanoi's efforts in the campaign against Falconi and his men.

"Now that we know the Black Eagles have engaged the East Germans, what is our next step?" Truong asked.

"We must draw them farther north to get within reach of General Vang Ngoc's troops," Krashchenko answered.

"It almost seems as if we're sending a water buffalo to destroy a mouse," Truong said. "Wouldn't a small cat do just as well? Surely the East German and his men, with support from the local Viet Cong, are enough to successfully conclude this entire situation."

"Hardly," Krashchenko replied testily. He disliked having his decisions and plans questioned by Truong; in the racist Soviet society, Oriental minorities are not given much opportunity for criticism or suggestion. "Falconi and his men have proven that they hardly fit the description of mice. And I would like to emphasize that troops from your own army, though outnumbering the Black Eagle devils, have been soundly beaten by them on no less then three occasions."

Truong hid his anger at this obvious insult behind his placid expression. He held up the recently arrived message. "Excuse me, but I must point out that this latest word also informs us that Stahler lost half the men with him in this latest clash with Falconi. It would appear that Europeans are faring no better than my own people."

Krashchenko, who didn't want to go too far in putting down his NVA counterpart, displayed a more benevolent attitude. "You're right, of course. But when we are able to get Vang's command into the fight, then your army will be the main participant in the Black Eagles' destruction."

"It will be an honor for Vang," Truong said. "Particularly in light of the fact that his last contact with Falconi resulted in his disgrace. He is well motivated with genuine hatred. You need not worry about any lack of effectiveness or dedication on his part."

Krashchenko nodded his agreement. "I know. Now we must formulate the plans for both Trang and Stahler in pulling the Black Eagles closer to us. As soon as they are in the most convenient place we will make our final moves against him."

"I appreciate your confidence," Truong said.

"Mark my words, Comrade," Krashchenko said, smiling, "the day is near that Falconi will be standing as a prisoner in this very office."

Clayton Andrews, with Chuck Fagin and Andrea Thuy at his side, walked behind the young ARVN staff officer who escorted them down the hall of the heavily guarded South Vietnamese Army Headquarters' second floor. They came to a door watched over by no less then two sentries and a sergeant. After the noncom checked all credentials — including their escort's — they were admitted to the room on the other side.

This was the domain of Colonel Ngai Quang. His large staff, expecting the callers, were gathered in a group. One of them spoke softly into an intercom. Within moments Ngai appeared from a nearby office. He looked at the three callers and smiled a greeting.

Clayton Andrews bowed slightly. "Good afternoon, Colonel Ngai."

Ngai approached and offered his hand. "How are you today, Mister Andrews?"

"I am fine, thank you." He indicated his companions. "You are, of course, acquainted with Mister Fagin and Lieutenant Thuy."

"Yes," Ngai answered still smiling.

"Mister Fagin has something he would like to say to you, Colonel."

Ngai feigned surprise. "Really? And what might that be?"

Chuck Fagin had received the radio message telling him of Sergeant Jack Galchaser's death only a couple of hours previously. Despite his emotional turmoil over the unhappy event, he kept his face locked in an impassive expression. He stepped forward. "Colonel Ngai, I wish to offer you my apologies for the impolite way I treated you on the several occasions that you called on me at my office. My conduct was discourteous and thoughtless. I am truly sorry."

Ngai, his grin widening, spoke loudly. "I accept your apology, Mister Fagin. I hope this marks a new and friendly beginning to our working relationship."

"I'm sure it will," Fagin said coldly.

Andrea Thuy stepped forward and stood at attention. "And I, *Dại Tá* Ngai, also wish to beg your forgiveness for my disrespectful conduct toward you. I apologize."

"And I regret any hasty words I may have spoken to you, *Trung Úy* Thuy," Ngai said magnanimously. "Your service to our republic is beyond measure."

"Cám o'n ông, Dại Ta," Andrea said.

With the public apology given and Ngai's Oriental temperament soothed, his staff returned to their desks and the work that awaited them.

"Won't you all come into my office for some refreshments?" Ngai asked.

"Delighted," Andrews said.

The ARVN colonel's work area was actually two chambers. The outer one was a sitting room complete with sofas and a coffee table. As they made themselves comfortable, an orderly pushing a tea cart appeared. He wordlessly served them and placed a plate of baked refreshments on the table before leaving.

"Please help yourselves," Ngai offered, taking a sip of tea.

"Thank you," Andrews said, choosing a chocolate donut. "We realize you're a very busy man, Colonel, so we won't take up a lot of your time. Mister Fagin has prepared a briefing to bring you completely up to date on the latest activities and personnel of the Black Eagles Detachment." He glanced at Fagin. "Would you care to begin now?"

"Of course," Fagin said. He reached into his coat pocket and withdrew a set of notes. "At this time, Major Robert Falconi and his men are involved in a special operation west of Danang."

"Excuse me, Mister Fagin," Ngai interrupted. "Could you show me their *exact* location on my wall map?"

Fagin hesitated, but he answered, "I would be happy

to."

"Thank you," Ngai said settling back as Fagin began a full disclosure.

Horny Galchaser's death hit the Black Eagles especially hard.

Not only had he been an original member of the group, but as a dedicated father and family man, he had gotten a lot of respect from his friends who were used to womanizers among married professional soldiers. The sobering thought in every man's mind was how Betty Jean Galchaser and the three kids would take the loss.

And his body was in enemy hands too.

The fight with the Caucasian renegades had seemed like a victory at first. But when the surprise attack by the Viet Cong guerrillas swept into the battle, the overwhelmed Black Eagles were forced into an ignominious retreat. The successful break in contact and withdrawal to a safer area could be credited mostly to Master Sergeant Top Gordon.

Top had coordinated the movement and support between both fire teams while Falconi had concentrated on directing the fighting. Neither Falconi nor his senior NCO had received much help from Dinky Dow. The Vietnamese had forgotten his command responsibilities during the heat of battle. He'd also demonstrated a marked increase in his irrational attitude, brought on by constant exposure to the pressures of combat. Falconi was beginning to become seriously worried about the ex-VC's mental condition.

Now, the day after the battle, the detachment was in a jungle ravine, easily defensable and hidden, resting up before their next effort.

Falconi held a council of war with Top and Dinky Dow while Sparks Jackson and Archie Dobbs waited off a short distance. The major didn't like either his scout or radio operator to get too far away from him.

Lightfingers O'Quinn had been taken out of Bravo Team and placed in with the Alphas who had suffered both casualties. The team also was short of fire support since Horny had been killed. The circumstances of the battle had resulted in the M-79 grenade launcher being lost with his body.

Falconi sucked on a blade of grass. "We still don't know who those white men are, but we did manage to kill nine or ten of 'em in my estimation."

"Yeah," Top agreed. "I just wish we knew how many there were for sure. Makes it hard to formulate plans."

"Never mind bullshit," Dinky Dow said. "We find the bastards and kick ass."

"The simplest approach is best sometimes," Falconi admitted, "but not in these circumstances, Dinky Dow. There's too many unknown factors here. Like who, how many, and where to mention a few."

"I suppose," Dinky Dow agreed reluctantly. "But we always do good when we fight, Falcon. So we should make fight—that's all—just make fight."

"I don't know enough about what's going on to keep this operation going now," Falconi said.

"Seems like the classical spot for a detailed reconnaissance patrol," Top remarked.

"Mmmm," Falconi mused. "Or a combination recon and combat effort."

Top raised his eyebrows in anticipation. "You got something in mind, Skipper?"

"Yeah." Falconi motioned over at Archie. "Come here

a minute, Sport."

"You bet," Archie said, getting to his feet and ambling over. "You call, I haul . . . that's all! He settled down with the others. "What's up?"

"You, Dinky Dow, and I are going for a little promenade and look-see out in the deep dark forest," Falconi said. "I want to locate those outlaws, identify 'em and also lay some hurt on the bastards if possible."

"Hot damn!" Dinky Dow exclaimed. "Kick ass!"

"Right," Falconi said. "But in a subtle kind of way. We'll travel lean and mean, so leave most of your gear here. The main thing I want to do is locate them, then bring the detachment back and wrap this episode up." He glanced at Master Sergeant Gordon. "Top, you're in charge. Keep the home fires burning 'til we get back."

"Right, Skipper."

Archie looked thoughtful. "Lemme get this straight. We're going into enemy territory to look for some strange guys, right? We don't know where they are, who they are or how many of them there are. But we're gonna find out all this and kick some ass in the bargain, huh?"

"Right," Falconi answered. "If the situation warrants, that is. We may just be able to poke around and then have to come back for the other guys before we can do 'em any harm."

Archie grinned. "Either way it sounds like fun, Skipper. When do we leave?"

Falconi shucked most of his gear and stood up with pistol belt, pistol, knife, canteen, and ammo. His M-16 was slung over his shoulder. "Let's hit the road."

The 327th Infantry Battalion was not the most elite in

the NVA—North Vietnamese Army. But it was well motivated for the job it had been assigned.

A few months ago the outfit had been a freshly organized, group of enthusiastic young soldiers and dedicated officers preparing to make a great contribution to the Communists' plans for conquering the southern part of Vietnam. After months of training, it had been sent to the western jungle to put a cutting edge on its combat effectiveness with a final few weeks of maneuvers and exercises before commitment to combat.

It was the battalion's bad luck to be in the exact area of an objective assigned to the Black Eagles. When the raiders hit the prison camp in the vicinity of the 327th's headquarters, its commander Major Dai Vo responded with an all-out effort to destroy or capture the attackers.

He and many of his men died in this futile effort.

Other elements of the NVA, under the command of General Vang Ngoc, were then assigned to smash the invaders. During the last stages of the operation, even with the Black Eagles trapped with their backs to the mighty Song Bo River, everything had gone to hell for the Reds. The raiders not only managed to escape to freedom in the south, they inflicted even more casualties on the North Vietnamese.

Vang was in disgrace. As a general he had commanded an entire brigade of troops, but now, because of his failure on the Song Bo, his command had been reduced to a mere batallion—the miserable 327th.

Less than a month previously, he and his men had been sent to Laos where the Black Eagles were operating against the Pathet Lao. But the fates were again unkind, allowing the American Falconi to elude capture or death and to pull back to safety within his own lines.

Now, after weeks and weeks of edging south in an overall master plan to draw the Black Eagles within striking distance, they had reached a point in the vicinity of the dividing line between North and South Vietnam. And they had gotten the word to prepare for imminent contact with the very men who had shamed and embarrassed them.

Vang sat in his palm-thatched field shelter, munching on his meager ration of rice balls. He had received word via radio that Captain Stahler and his East German contingent had made contact with the Black Eagles. The Russian KGB officer Krashchenko had set a scheme into motion—one that would bring Falconi into their midst.

Vang wiped his mouth and glanced at his adjutant. "We are drawing closer to our prey."

"Perhaps it would be wiser to suggest they are drawing closer to us, Comrade General," the young captain suggested. He had been nervous when he'd found himself assigned as Vang's adjutant. The general was in serious trouble and facing possible punishment over losing the battle on the Song Bo. But now, after several months, the adjutant was more at ease. Vang was an old campaigner who had survived other setbacks—both militarily and politically—before. This latest situation, in which he had been assigned a command beneath his rank, was beginning to look as if it would turn into a glorious accomplishment.

"No matter whether we are hunters or merely a trap," Vang said with conviction. "I have every intention of serving up the American Falconi on a platter to General Headquarters in Hanoi."

CHAPTER TWELVE

The earth's terrain, to the properly attuned tracker, is as readable as a book.

Sergeant Archie Dobbs, of the Black Eagles Detachment, was just such an individual. Despite being born and raised in the concrete womb of Boston, Archie possessed a talent that had lain dormant within his being until his entry into the army and subsequent exposure to the primitive outdoors.

Archie was a born tracker and pathfinder.

If he had come into the world a couple of hundred years previously, the intrepid young soldier would have been among the first to break across the Appalachian or Allegheny Mountains and move west to explore the dangerous wilderness that spread out from the narrow seaboard of civilization across the unknown sprawl of the American continent. Archie's ancestors, who had arrived in the colonies during the times when such activities were feasible, had been prevented from becoming pioneers due to the circumstances of their arrival.

They had come in chains, released from English

prisons as bonded servants—virtual slaves to the people who held the papers on them. Any attempt to leave the supervision and control of their masters was a serious crime. Confused and locked into a cruel system, they had bided their time. When the terms of enslavement ended, they chose to remain within the confines of familiar territory rather than wander off. After a couple of generations, the former bonded servants, through circumstances brought on by the industrial revolution, were caught up in the manufacturing syndrome and life-style of the East coast.

Thus, the Dobbs—like many other families—donated several generations to the mills and factories of Massachusetts.

Archie's older ancestors in England had been involved in more romantic activities to earn their bread. In fact, it was because of their mode of making a living that they ended up in the English judicial system that eventually sold then into bondage in the colonies.

The Dobbs family were poachers.

No earl, duke, lord of a manor, or even king of England could keep the persistent Dobbs clan from hunting and fishing their private domains. Generations of following this dangerous trade had developed genes in which all the necessary skills of stealth, tracking, and directional orientation had evolved to the maximum.

These talents were combined with stubbornness, fearlessness too.

To this day in the English county of Nottinghamshire, there is the tale out of the misty past which involves a man named Dobbs who, rather than shrieking in agony while being drawn and quartered, shouted of how he had enjoyed a certain lord's roasted venison—the very crime for which he was being so painfully executed.

Now the scion of that great line of interloping out-doorsmen, unaware of where his natural talents came from, crouched while studying the soft ground of the Vietnamese jungle. He noted the bent direction of the blades of grass and the amount they had risen since being trampled. Grass is flexible and eventually regains its original position after being stepped on. How much it recovers, depends on the amount of time elapsed since it was disturbed, its type, and the weather conditions—all factors well known to Archie Dobbs.

He also noted the angle at which several snapped twigs had been driven into the ground. He looked up at his commanding officer.

"They went this way all right, Skipper," Archie said.

"You're sure they're the white guys, not any VC?" Falconi asked.

"It's those bastards all right," the scout said. "This scuffing was made by GI boots. But there's a coupla lightweights wearin' sandals."

"Probably their VC guides," Falconi said.

"Yeah," Archie agreed. He studied the almost invisible markings a few moments more. "They must've come through here about two or three hours ago."

"Okay," Falconi acknowledged with full confidence. "Let's keep on their asses then."

"Right, Skipper." Archie rose and resumed his silent traveling with the Falcon and Dinky Dow following.

The Vietnamese delivery driver opened the back of the truck and pulled the clothes out, dropping them into a small cart. Then he wheeled the conveyance inside the dry cleaning plant located on Tan Son Nhut Air Force

Base.

The establishment, though primarily for the use of American personnel, was preferred by the rich and elite portion of Saigon's citizens. The quality of the work done was definitely superior to that of the local cleaners.

The clothing was carefully bundled and tagged to indicate its owners. The driver sorted through the items, preparing them to be sent into the cleaning area. When he reached the pile bearing the name of Colonel Ngai Quang, the man gave them particular attention.

One of Ngai's tunics, a distinctive American model, was closely examined by the driver. He fingered the bottom seam and could barely feel the tightly rolled tissue paper there. A quick glance around the room showed that none of the other workers there was paying him much attention. The Vietnamese pulled the paper free and deftly shoved it into the folds of his own loose shirt.

After putting the soiled clothes into the proper bins, the man went to shipping to pick up his next delivery. As usual, he had the downtown run where wealthy Vietnamese merchants received their freshly cleaned business suits for quick changes in the hot, humid weather.

One of these customers was Tsing Chai, owner of a gambling parlor.

The driver, after again making sure he was unobserved, took the paper and inserted it into the cardboard tube on the hanger holding one of Tsing's western suits. Then, with the rest of his delivery, he loaded it into his truck for the run into Saigon's commercial and sin districts.

Archie, crouching behind the bush, signaled a cautioning gesture back to Falconi and Dinky Dow. Then he pointed up the faint trail.

Falconi carefully and slowly assumed a standing position behind the tree he was using for concealment. It took him only a moment to spot the object of Archie's attention. He squatted down again and leaned toward Dinky Dow's ear. "Two VC," he whispered. "I'll let the first go past—you take him."

"Right, Falcon," Dinky Dow said with a gleam in his eye. He pulled his boot knife as he lowered his M-16 to the ground. "You gonna take second motherfucker?"

"Yeah."

The two Reds, careless in their ignorance of danger, strode down the path a couple of meters apart. Having guided the East Germans to their camp, the pair was on the way back to report to their own leader. The second, fatigued and inattentive, walked carelessly and rather noisily behind his companion. Only when Dinky Dow appeared on the path and made a silent attack on his friend, did the VC's mind leap back to wakefulness.

But Falconi's strong arm and sharp knife ended all consciousness . . . then life for the guerrilla.

Two blades bit into living flesh, and two Charlies writhed in the throes of their skillfully administered deaths. Within moments their final shudders announced their departure from earthly cares and wants.

The two Black Eagles dragged their dead quarry back out of sight into the bushes. Archie joined them after brushing away all telltale tracks and scuff marks from the dirt on the trail. "Them two coulda fucked up our mission," he remarked.

"Good thing you saw 'em," Falconi said. "How far is the base camp?"

"No more'n a coupla hunnerd meters, Skipper," Archie answered. "But we're gonna have to move slower'n hell to get there. Could be more VC wanderin' around here."

"Okay," Falconi said. "Let's take our time then. All I want to do in daylight hours is take a good look at the lay of their area. Then I'll decide what we'll do after dark."

The trio avoided the trail, moving into the more difficult, but safer, area of the jungle. Each step had to be taken with extreme care. A single careless movement, no matter how slight, could result in their discovery by any nearby listening or observation posts. It took them three hours to travel a distance of two hundred meters. By the time they had located a safe area from which to look into the camp, it was already late afternoon.

Falconi was impressed with the neatness of the place. The huts, while primitive, were laid out in an orderly fashion. The ground between them, even at that exact moment, was being methodically swept with palm fronds by a couple of native orderlies of sorts. One of the white strangers, standing in the door of a hut, spoke to the two workers. His words, while faint, were discerned by Falconi:

"Ich möchte diesen Areal gereinigt durchaus und mit schnell!"

The two Vietnamese, obviously unable to understand, appeared frightened of the man. But they evidently sensed his meaning and redoubled their efforts.

"Damn!" Falconi whispered to his companions. "The son of a bitch is a Kraut."

"What the hell would any Squareheads be doin' in Vietnam?" Archie asked.

"Exactly what these bastards are up to," Falconi answered. "Making us look bad by playing like they're Americans."

138

"Prob'ly East Germans then, huh?" Dobbs said.

"No matter," Dinky Dow said. "Kill the motherfuckers. Kick East German ass!"

"Ease up, Dinky Dow," Falconi said. The strain of combat was relentlessly threatening to destroy the little Vietnamese's already precarious mental balance. "Getting those bastards is the main idea behind our mission," Falconi said. "But there's not much the three of us can do right now." He glanced up at the waning sun. "It'll be dark soon. We've got to put as much distance between ourselves and them as we can before we have to settle in for the night. I want to bring the rest of the detachment up here and end this operation on a grand scale — with prisoners."

"Right, Skipper," Archie said in agreement. "Let's shag ass now."

"I say we kill some motherfuckers!" Dinky Dow hissed. His eyes seemed glazed over.

"We'll do that," Falconi said in a soothing voice. "But we have to wait for the right time. Okay?"

"Shit!" Dinky Dow said. He appeared to grow agitated, but he quickly settled down. Then he shrugged. "Okay."

The three Black Eagles pulled back into the vegetation, then turned to retrace their steps to where Top Gordon and the rest of the detachment waited for them.

The streetlights were already on as the dry cleaning truck pulled up to the curb in front of Tsing Chai's mahjongg parlor. The driver, in near coolie fashion, scurried around to the back and pulled several items of clothing from the vehicle's racks. Then he trotted up to the front entrance. He bobbed his head in a servile manner at the burly Chinese doorman who guarded the entrance to the gambling establishment.

"Clean clothes for Master Tsing," he announced with a humble smile.

He went inside and dodged apologetically through the crowd of patrons. When he arrived at a curtained portal he stopped again. There were two heavyweight Oriental types there.

"Please," the driver said bowing. "I have clothes for Master Tsing."

One of the guards glared with open contempt at the skinny little Vietnamese. He was tempted to take the items from him and to send the miserable little insect stumbling back outside with a couple of well-placed kicks, but there were explicit orders regarding dry cleaning deliveries.

"Go on in and don't waste a lot of Master Tsing's time!" he snapped.

"Oh, I shall be as fast as possible, yes. Thank you, sir!"

The driver hastened through the curtains and down to another door. He knocked timidly. "Master Tsing! Master Tsing! The dry cleaning is here, please!"

A few moments later Tsing admitted him. When the driver was in, the fat Chinese shut the door. Then he bowed respectfully to the driver. "I bid you welcome again, Comrade *Dai'Uy* Xong."

Xong wordlessly pulled Tsing's suit from the hanger and flung it at him. Then he removed the rolled-up tissue paper and went over to the desk to spread the document out. He rapidly read it, then turned his attention back to Tsing. "It is another change in the location of the Black Eagles' operational position. This must be relayed to Comrade Colonel Krashchenko as quickly as possible."

"Yes, Comrade *Dai'Uy* Xong," Tsing said. "I will have it encoded and transmitted immediately."

As the Chinese went out the office, Xong helped himself to a soft drink at the wet bar in one corner of the room. A captain in North Vietnamese intelligence, he had been operating in South Vietnam since the French withdrawal some ten years previously. He had concentrated on maintaining a cover of humble, almost demeaning jobs as he moved through the fluctuating world where South Vietnamese society came into contact with foreign elements. Thus, through establishing a good work record, he was eventually able to get a job considered quite desirable by working Vietnamese — delivery driver for the air base dry cleaners.

Xong was on his second cola when Tsing reappeared. The gambling hall operator again bowed. "The message has been transmitted and its receipt properly acknowledged per proper procedures, Comrade *Dai'Uy* Xong."

"Very well, Comrade Tsing," Xong said taking a seat at the Chinese man's own desk. "It would appear that Comrade Krashchenko's plan is working quite well. The Black Eagles are indeed traveling north toward the border of the people's republic. Within a few days or a week they should be within striking distance of Comrade *Thiêú Tu'ón'g* Vang and the 327th Battalion."

"That will be the end of those gangsters," Tsing said

"Ngai has informed us that they have suffered two casualties already," Xong continued in an almost gloating manner. "That puts their total strength down to ten effectives."

"And how many of our brave comrades are serving in

the 327th?" Tsing asked.

"I would estimate the strength to be of approximately four hundred men," Xong said. He held up his empty glass. "I will have another. And pour one for yourself as well."

"Yes, Comrade *Dai Uy*," Tsing said. *"Cám o'n ông!* Thank you very much." He tended to the task rapidly and returned Xong's drink to him. He held up his own. "Here's to the final victory over the Black Eagles!"

"With odds of four hundred to ten—make that forty to one—I feel it safe to expect our goals regarding the brigand Falconi will be accomplished quite quickly and with undeniable finality."

The two Communist agents drank the toast. Then Xong, without another word, set his glass down. He went back through the door and, upon reaching the curtained exit, scurried through and dodged among the gamblers on the way back to his delivery truck.

Once again he was the servile little errand boy.

CHAPTER THIRTEEN

The cobra was disturbed. His hunting grounds had been violated on several occasions during the previous twenty-four hours. The serpent, used to being feared and avoided by other animals, sensed a danger in these strange beings that had moved into his domain.

Not only were they large, but they seemed a deadly species with strange powers of a sort that the large snake felt he could not overcome. Reacting to his small brain's warnings, the reptile moved away from the source of his uneasiness to wait out the situation in a safer area.

Nearby, unaware of the snake's retreat, Master Sergeant Top Gordon crawled up beside Chun Kim. He nodded silently to the Korean marine and checked the field of fire offered to the man's M-79 grenade launcher.

"Looking good here," Top said.

"You betcha!" Kim agreed. He pointed at a hut larger than the others. "I think that my first target, no?"

"Right," Top said. "Hit 'em with a couple of rounds there, then swing over to the hut two down from the left."

"Okay, Top. Look like a headquarters, huh?"

"Yeah, or at least an orderly room of some sort." The team sergeant got to his feet. "I'm going to check the others, but I'll be back before the attack starts. You and I'll move in together."

Wordlessly, he withdrew to visit the other posts of Bravo Fire Team.

Top found Malpractice McCorckel set up and ready a short distance away. As usual, the medic had been chosen as the group's automatic rifleman. He was, in effect, a poor man's machine gunner. With his M-16 set on full auto, he would sweep the target area in an effort to aid Kim's 40-millimeter grenade barrages.

"You ready for the blast off?" Top asked him.

Malpractice winked and patted the extra bandoleer of ammo over his shoulder. "That resupply drop Lightfingers arranged did the job."

"We were lucky," Top said candidly.

The day before, after Falconi, Archie, and Dinky Dow had returned from their reconnaissance, they had arranged for a drop directly into the jungle. Its bundles, with only small drag chutes to slow them, had crashed blindly through the trees. The success of the small operation had depended on grid coordinates derived from highly accurate map reading. Combining these with unerring piloting on the part of the air force had resulted in a successful reprovisioning. Everyone had done his job and now, with a fresh influx of ammo and C-rations, the Black Eagles were poised in their attack positions just outside the East Germans' camp.

Top Gordon's next call was on Calvin Culpepper. He sensed the husky, black demolitions sergeant was sinking into a morale problem. He squatted down beside him and pulled a couple of cigarettes from his pocket. "Want a blue-label, Calvin?" he asked offering him a PX-bought cigarette. They were among the last he had. A couple more and Top would be reduced to smoking the dried-up C-ration fags.

Calvin took the cigarette. After lighting it and the one Top had taken, he silently settled back and surveyed his area of responsibility out to his immediate front.

"Looks like you got a good position," Top remarked. "Malpractice is on your right and Lightfingers is ready and raring to go to the left."

"Yeah," Calvin said. "I wonder how long they'll last — or me too."

Top knew that Horny's death was affecting Calvin more than he'd been letting on. "Tough to lose a pal," he remarked. "God knows I've done it enough times. I guess it's just a part of soldiering."

"It's gotta be the worstest part of army life," Calvin said. He smoked in silence for several moments, then he began talking. "Of the original thirteen guys that started up the Black Eagles we've already lost eight of 'em. And that don't count the dudes that's been attached or assigned later. All in all, there's been eighteen guys zapped on our operations."

Top was surprised that Calvin had been keeping such close count. "We're in a dangerous business. I took the old team sergeant's place, remember?"

"Yeah . . . Sergeant Snow," Calvin said. "He got killed on his second mission." He ground out the cigarette on the ground in front of him. "That was the bad 'un . We got caught between the Mau Xanh and Song Bo Rivers. Took a lotta casualties, Top. Ever'thing from mortar fire and small arms right to Mig air strikes on

145

our asses. All of us nearly bought the farm then."

Top tried desperately to think of something to say. The combination of ceaseless missions with no R&R and the death of friends was enough to destroy the Black Eagles despite their high morale and motivation. "We'll be getting a break after this."

"Horny already got his," Calvin said. "And so did Tommy Newcomb. Matter o' fact, if it hadn't been for Tommy we'd of all got killed or captured on the Song Bo. Him and some of his Australian SAS buddies had been runnin' ops with local tribesmen in the area. They covered our withdrawal across the river. Tommy was assigned to the Black Eagles after that. Then his luck went to shit."

"It'll work out," Top said. "I got to report in to the Falcon, Cal. I'll talk to you later."

"Right, Top," Calvin said dejectedly. "Have a nice day."

"Yeah."

Top Gordon left his team and reported in to Falconi at his hastily chosen command post. It was a typical CP for the Black Eagles' commander. It was established by the mere act of his sitting down and issuing orders. The detachment sergeant, his M-16 slung over his shoulder, stood in front of Falconi. "The Bravos are ready, Skipper. At least as much as can be expected."

"Sounds like you got a problem, Top," Falconi remarked.

"*We* got a problem," Top corrected him. "Morale is rapidly sinking. Horny's death is affecting the old guys. Malpractice hasn't said much, but it's obvious just the same. Calvin is really down in the dumps."

"So's Lightfingers," Falconi added. "I've just been

talking with him over future resupply operations, and his heart just isn't in it." He sighed. "Dinky Dow isn't much help in that area. All the crazy little bastard wants to do is fight. He doesn't take time to consider anything else."

"I noticed that too, Skipper," Top said. "He's a hell of a man in combat, but when it comes to being an executive officer or team leader, he comes up short."

"We've got problems all right, Top," Falconi acknowledged. He was glad to have this opportunity to use Gordon as a detachment sergeant. "And they won't be solved until we can pull out of active ops and do some reorganizing and resting up."

"That goddamned Fagin's got to be taken down a notch or two," Gordon said. He made the statement more out of a desire to draw Falconi out of his own shell than as a criticism of the CIA case officer.

"Fagin's okay," the major said. "You got to remember he's more of a staff intelligence man than a combat leader. Most of his assignments have been in clandestine spying. He's had little actual contact with the enemy since he left the OSS at the end of World War II. He's following his gut reasoning when he keeps us off R&R. I think the guy's apprehensions are all fucked up, but at least his intentions are good."

"Screw him, Skipper," Gordon said. "If he doesn't want us in Saigon, then let him ship us somewhere else. Or at least find some safe house where he can settle the guys in with liquor and whores for a few weeks."

"That'll be my first priority after this," Falconi said. He checked his watch. "We're jumping off in ten minutes, Top. You'd best get back to your team."

"Right, Skipper." He walked away, then suddenly remembered Calvin Culpepper's last words. He turned and looked at Falconi "Have a nice day."

Falconi looked at his detachment sergeant and winked. "I'll tell you what, Top," he said. "I'll do my damndest, okay?"

"What more could I ask of you, Skipper?"

Rolf Stahler peered from his hut as young Leutnant Willi Feldhaus strode across the compound toward him. Stahler smiled to himself despite the discomfort of the heat. Feldhaus appeared to be leading a regimental parade.

"How do things looks, Willi?" Stahler asked as his deputy commander stepped under the thatched roof.

"*Sehr gut, Kamerad Hauptmann.*" Feldhaus. said. He dropped into the foxhole. Each hut in the East German camp, rather than being a simple dwelling as it appeared, covered a two-man fighting hole. "As soon as the gangsters hit us, we'll be ready."

"It may be a bit difficult for the men to stay on alert status, but it can't be avoided at this point," Stahler said.

"Are you sure those *Schwarzenadler* are out there?" Feldhaus asked.

"Of course, Willi," Stahler answered. "I don't know exactly where, but there's no doubt that they've been committed into tracking us down. Certainly, this camp is too obvious for even the most unskillful jungle fighters to miss. And that description certainly doesn't fit Falconi and his men."

"I suppose they're bursting with curiosity about who we are," Feldhaus said.

"By now they are completely informed," Stahler said. "I reached that conclusion when the Viet Cong reported that the guides they provided hadn't returned. No doubt the unfortunate *Indo-Chinesin* were caught in a silent ambush of some kind. Falconi or some of his men have had this bivouac under surveillance."

"But perhaps the two missing Viet Cong deserted; perhaps they weren't killed or captured," Feldhaus suggested.

"I doubt that," Stahler mused. "At any rate, it doesn't concern us one way or the other. What is important right now is the proximity of the *Schwarzenadler* and how soon they will attack."

Feldhaus nodded. "*Ja!* But we are ready for the *Schweine.*"

Top Gordon's ear was pressed so tight into the Prick-Six radio that it ached. He was relieved to hear Falconi's short but meaningful transmission:

"Go for it!"

The detachment sergeant tapped Chun Kim on the shoulder. Kim, who had maintained a careful sight picture on his first target, pulled the trigger of the M-79. It coughed and spat out the grenade which made a slight arch before crashing into the large hut in the bivouac's center. He quickly followed this up with two more while M-16 fire raked the huts.

Dinky Dow leaped from his concealment and charged into the open area at the edge of the East German's camp. He fired several quick fusillades into the nearest huts. Popeye Jenkins, not too far away, backed up the Alpha Team leader's efforts with a few shots of his own.

They were rewarded with the sight of two men scrambling out the back of their crude dwelling and streaking to another some twenty meters away.

Popeye took careful aim on the farthest one and pulled the trigger of his M-16. The man, hit between the shoulder blades, went down and made an undignified somersault. His companion leaped over him, then dove through the roof of the nearest hut. Several volleys erupted from the structure. Dinky Dow, with spurts of dirt flying around his running feet, quickly sought cover behind the abandoned position.

On the other side of the line, Top Gordon and his Bravo team began their sweep into the camp. Malpractice's steady bursts of full automatic fire rhythmically punctuated the explosions of Chun Kim's grenades. The Alphas advanced cautiously as the East Germans methodically pulled back from them.

One young defender, however, with more aggression than good sense, turned in a gesture of bravado. He fired two quick shots at Kim who ignored him to continue his support mission. The Red, noting the situation, stopped his hasty firing and took the time to aim steady and long.

Calvin Culpepper performed his own sharpshooting exhibition a split-second faster. He got a classic, sight picture on the German's head and gently squeezed the trigger of his rifle. The bullet rocketed into the enemy soldier's head with such force the young man appeared to be a puppet on a string suddenly jerked by an impatient child, then flung to the ground.

Calvin pumped three additional rounds into the twitching body. He caught up with Kim and fired several more shots to give the Korean a chance to reload without receiving rounds from enemy positions.

From his location in the center of the attack, Falconi could follow the battle's developments with ease. He noted the East Germans had begun pulling back almost immediately when the fight began. They seemed to be withdrawing in a preplanned methodical sense. The Black Eagle commander was glad to note that Top Gordon was maintaining close control on his Bravo Team and seeing to it that their fire-and-maneuver technique was flawless and well coordinated.

Dinky Dow was another story.

The feisty little Vietnamese had followed his old practice of turning from soldier to warrior once the fighting was under way. His team—Archie Dobbs, Popeye Jenkins, and Lightfingers O'Quinn—moved forward in a steadily disintegrating formation. The Alphas, for all intents and purposes, were a rudderless boat, drifting on the waves of circumstance.

Falconi jumped into command. "Popeye," he yelled at the sailor who occupied the middle of the team. "Go on full auto and sweep the area in front of Archie and Lightfingers."

Without hesitating, Popeye flipped the selector switch of the M-16 and went to work.

"Bring it up, Lightfingers," Falconi yelled. "Keep aligned with the Bravos." He turned. "Archie—"

"I know, Skipper," the scout yelled back. "I'll keep an eye on Lightfingers."

Now, in cohesion with the Bravos, the Alphas moved forward as the last of the East Germans retreated from the battle and pulled out under the covering fire of their comrades already at the tree line.

The Black Eagles advanced to the farthest positions. They occupied the fighting holes that were now abandoned.

Falconi was aware he was outnumbered. There had

been at least thirty East Germans in the bivouac at the start of the attack. Although three of them now lay sprawled on the small battlefield, the survivors still had a numerical advantage of almost three to one over Falconi and his men. A counterattack seemed likely.

There was nothing to do at that point, but to see what would develop.

The cobra slithered back into his hunting grounds. He raised up and spread his hood as a warning to any potential attackers, but his flickering tongue could perceive no body heat from other beings.

However, he did sense the blood and death that wafted on the slight breeze around him.

Whatever killing had been done here was beyond the serpent's comprehension. He could understand death for the sake of eating or defense, but here there had been another kind — more violent and wanton than anything he could imagine.

Feeling uneasy at such horror, the cobra withdrew into the denser bushes nearby.

CHAPTER FOURTEEN

Le Quartier des Colons was a unique neighborhood —
even for an exotic and unusual city like Saigon.

It was a dingy, run-down area walled off by its own
dilapidated apartment houses and building establish-
ments. Entrance to the vicinity was made through several gates that had evolved between the buildings.
Thus, Le Quartier des Colons was not unlike a rather
run-down walled city within a city.

The inhabitants of the neighborhood were expatriates
from France. They had once been part of the great empire, serving in various capacities in the military, the
civil service, or in some other part of the bureaucracy
that administered French Indochina in the old days.
After the Battle of Dien Bien Phu in 1954 when both
North and South Viet Nam had been set up as independent countries, many of these colonials had returned to
the country of their birth. But only a short stay in La
Belle République was enough to convince them they
had become strangers in their native regions. With so
many years away from former customs and traditions

they could never become regular Frenchmen again; they were irretrievably *colons* — colonials — for the rest of their days.

They had returned to Saigon to live in the past. These lost Frenchmen remembered days of colonial grandeur and authority. The *colons* had been on top of the heap then. They had ruled this humid, hot land, living in relative luxury, enjoying the best housing, food, drink, and women the region had to offer.

Now most of them were on the border of poverty. The ones who were best off existed on the meager pensions they had earned during their long years of service. Other held minor jobs in the South Vietnamese government or had their own less than lucrative businesses in the Quartier.

Chuck Fagin sat on the sidewalk under the awning of such an establishment. It was an outdoor café and bar where the owner, a fat, hairy former supervisor of native motor mechanics, served an indifferent cuisine. The faded clientele sipped a particularly bad *vin rouge* to drown the poorly prepared food.

Fagin had chosen this spot as a place where a white man could sit in the reasonable expectation of not being disturbed or even particularly noticed. And, indeed, there were several *colons* lounging about the various tables in a display of rather shabby leisure. Fagin took a sip of the wine from the dirty glass, winced, then continued waiting.

After enduring another half glass of that truly awful product of the grape, Fagin was glad to see a dapper Vietnamese wearing a white suit approach. The man smiled a greeting and joined him.

"How are you, Mister Fagin?" The accent was crisp

despite being Oriental.

"I am fine, Colonel Tran," Fagin said. He noted the briefcase the man carried. "I presume you have the information I require of you?"

They were interrupted by the appearance of the proprietor. Ashes fell on his stained shirt front from the large, cheap cigar he chewed. "Do you require anything, *monsieur?*" he asked of the new arrival.

"No. Nothing, *merci,*" the Vietnamese said. He was a colonel in the national police, serving directly under the all-powerful General Nguyen Ngoc Loan.

The ex-Frenchman shrugged as if not too surprised and retreated back into the interior of his seedy café.

"Please examine the statements here," Tran said. "I must return them to my contact's bank office before the business day ends."

"Of course," Fagin said. He pulled a bound sheaf of papers from the small case. They were the latest, up-to-date financial statements regarding one Colonel Ngai Quang of the Army of South Vietnam.

Fagin wasn't interested in a complete, detailed account. All he wanted to see was what any laymen could understand—a list of deposits and withdrawals along with amounts in various checking and savings accounts. It only took him ten minutes to run through the figures. He handed the documents back to Tran. "Nothing unusual here."

"There would not seem to be, Mister Fagin," Tran said. "The amounts listed and the various transactions don't seem out of the ordinary for a man of Ngai's standing and background."

"I have to admit I'm disappointed," he said. "Did your surveillance reveal anything?"

"Yes," Tran answered. "And this may lead us to what you seem to suspect. Ngai is a gambler, Mister Fagin."

"He must win a little or break even most of the time," Fagin remarked. "His bank accounts are healthy, but don't have any large influx."

"The thing that is most confusing is that Ngai seems to lose constantly," Tran said. "And great amounts."

Fagin eyebrows arched. "Are you sure?"

"Positive," Tran answered. "I have a man in the mah-jongg parlor that Ngai frequents. He tells me the honorable colonel drops thousands of piasters on a regular basis."

"What other places does he frequent?" Fagin asked.

"None that we can discover," Tran said. "But it is certain that he is a heavy loser at a place owned by a Chinese refugee named Tsing Chai."

"And who is this Tsing Chai?"

"A member of Saigon's underworld," Tran answered. "He's a typical Chinese thug who's been in everything from prostitution to loan sharking. He got his start in a big way after escaping to here from China in 1948."

"That's when the Communists threw the Nationalists out, right?"

"Exactly," Tran answered. "Former businessmen and others living slightly illegal lives would not be looked on with favor by Mao's people. Many sought refuge in French Indochina."

"And I'm sure more than one agent snuck in here with them," Fagin remarked.

"Undoubtedly. A preliminary investigation of Tsing shows he arrived in Saigon with enough gold to establish himself in the gambling scene. As far as we know, that's all he's been doing."

"It is most odd for Ngai to be losing his ass all the time yet to display absolutely no financial ill effects from such disastrous gaming."

"You are right, Mister Fagin. My own curiosity has been aroused."

"Do you have any contacts on Ngai's staff?"

"I'm sorry. His security arrangements are most thorough."

"I see. Thank you, Colonel Tran," Fagin said getting up. "I would appreciate it if you would follow through on this investigation as far as you can."

"Of course, Mister Fagin."

"You'll be paid in the usual way," Fagin said, putting on his hat and stepping out from under the awning. "I hope to see you soon."

Tran smiled. "Thank you, Mister Fagin. And please don't worry. I have a good man on this case. Good-bye for now."

Betty Jean Galchaser was glad to have the job in the little dress shop on Bragg Boulevard. With the youngest of her three children now in school like his older brother and sister, time would have hung heavy on her hands during the day — especially with her husband Jack doing a tour in Viet Nam. This was an almost perfect way of waiting for his return. Rather than going back to their hometown in Oklahoma, Betty Jean preferred sticking close to the army during his overseas stint.

The store, located almost exactly between Fort Bragg, North Carolina, and the city of Fayetteville, was handy to her home in Bonnie Doones too. After packing the three children off to school, she had to make but a short drive and she was at work.

Betty had just finished with a customer and rung up the sale. After slipping the garment into a bag, she handed it over to the client. "Thank you so much. And please come back."

"You're welcome, Mrs. Galchaser. Have a real nice day."

Betty Jean watched the woman depart. At the same time she noted the taxi pulling up in front of the store. The driver got out of his vehicle and approached the shop door. He carried a small, yellow envelope in his hand.

Betty Jean's heart went cold.

The man stepped inside and spoke softly to another saleslady nearer the door. She pointed over at Betty Jean, and the man walked her way.

"No," Betty Jean said aloud. The man drew closer. "No! *No!*" She turned and fled through the back of the store and around the building.

She had known other wives of Special Forces troopers who had had cabbies call for them with those yellow envelopes — envelopes which bore telegrams that began:

THE DEPARTMENT OF DEFENSE REGRETS TO INFORM YOU . . .

Betty Jean reached her car before she realized she had left her purse with the keys behind. She stood there for a few moments with her hand on the door handle. After taking a few deep breaths, Betty Jean calmed down. She slowly loosened her grip and stepped back from the car, taking the small hanky from her front, dress pocket.

Betty Jean wiped her eyes, then returned to the interior of the store. She went up to the front. The man was still waiting for her.

"Mrs. Galchaser?"

"Yes." She held out her hand and took the telegram. Betty Jean didn't need to read it. She knew Jack was dead.

"They've shagged ass," Archie Dobbs reported after his reconnaissance patrol. "And that's no shit, Skipper."

Top Gordon and Dinky Dow glanced over at the detachment commander.

Falconi shook his head. "I can't quite see why," he mused. "The bastards outnumber us."

"I think they're hurting more than we realize," Top offered. "They haven't been that long out of Europe to be used to either this weather of this style of fighting, Skipper. Those Krauts are trained more in conventional warfare than the brand we employ out here."

"You could be right," Falconi conceded. "And we've yet to accomplish our mission. We've got four bodies, but no prisoners. We can't prove a goddamned thing to the world about American innocence in those atrocities without grabbing a couple of those guys alive and kicking."

"Let's get 'em," Dinky Dow said.

"We got no choice, really," Top said. "We go after 'em or pull out now."

"I've got to turn this over in my head," Falconi said. "You guys go get some rest." When the three started to leave, he stopped Dinky Dow. "I want to talk with you."

"Sure, Falcon," the Vietnamese said agreebly. "What can I do?"

"Listen to me, Dinky," Falconi said. "You're one of the best fighters in the detachment. But you're not leading your team worth a shit. You understand?"

Dinky Dow's eyes lowered. "Yes, Skipper. I forget my guys when the fight start. I sorry, but I can't help it."

"I know you don't do it on purpose," Falconi said. "There's a lot of hate in your heart for the VC and the NVA."

"You damn right, Falcon!"

"I'm taking you out of command," Falconi said. "I'm sorry. I have no choice."

Dinky Dow nodded. "It okay by me, Falcon. I understand. Maybe I make better scout anyhow. We in my home territory now. My old village pretty close."

"Okay. You'll take Archie's place and stay with me. I've got to completely reorganize the detachment. I'm going to let Top take over Alpha Team with Archie and Popeye in it. Sparks can join them too. There won't be too much radio traffic from us for a while now. Malpractice will have the Bravos with Kim and Calvin."

"Good idea, Falcon," Dinky Dow said happily. "Now I scout, huh? Okay. You gotta tell me. We go after East German motherfuckers?"

"Yeah," Falconi said grimly. "We're going after 'em."

The column of troops stepped lively despite their weariness. Their commander, General Vang, was observing them as they moved into position.

This was the 327th Infantry Battalion and they had been moving south for the previous two weeks. At first the rate of march had been easy, making it clear to even the most uninformed private soldier that there was no rush to reach whatever destination had been picked out for him.

Even when the battalion crossed from North into

South Vietnam, there had been no sense of urgency. The unit's political commissar had taken advantage of the situation to give them a stirring — or at least he thought so — speech. It was all about their finally arriving in the south where they would soon set about freeing their brother Vietnamese from the cruel yoke of right-wing tyranny placed across their shoulders by the land-owning aristocracy. These were the same oppressors that Uncle Ho and Uncle Giap had thrown out of the north with the French colonial gangsters.

But before the big job of liberating the south could get under way in the proper manner, there was another matter to deal with.

Each and every soldier of the 327th knew of the Black Eagles. They had carried on a long fight with those imperialist devils up near Dien Bien Phu. They had followed them south to be joined by other troops that finally trapped the running dogs of capitalism with the Song Bo River at their backs — but through some clever evil, the Black Eagles had managed to escape.

The soldiers of the 327th remembered this episode mainly because of the number of their friends who had been slaughtered during the fights with those gangsters. Even their beloved and dedicated commanding officer Comrade Major Dai Vo had died along with the unit's original commissar Comrade Major Hieu Lo Ren.

One of the most devastating episodes had occurred when the foreign devils had turned their own air strike against them. Comrade pilots flying Mig-17 fighters had been fooled into firing against their own NVA troops — the 327th to be exact. While a South Vietnamese who had stolen their radio, spoke over it to the airmen, the fliers were directed in sortie after sortie against the 327th's positions, causing hundreds of casualties.

But Comrade General Vang had taken command of them following all this. He had harangued them in sincere anger to exhort them to vengeance. The commissar had embellished the fiery speech with political and philosophical overtones until the troops were properly motivated.

Now, after moving into this new location, they had been told that the same devils—the Black Eagles—would soon be within reach. Valiant comrades from East Germany had come all the way from Europe to entice the pirates of the arch-criminal Falconi into their clutches.

Falconi, they were further told, was a Russian traitor. A typical Jew who used guile and terror to see to it that the goals of socialism were thwarted so he and his oily friends could manipulate world commerce and economics for their own gain by keeping the freedom-loving people of the world downtrodden in poverty and despair.

The troops of the 327th dug in. Even machine guns and mortars were placed in readiness while Vang organized flying groups of infantry that would be used to surround and contain the Black Eagles, offering them but two choices:

Surrender or die!

CHAPTER FIFTEEN

The *dojo* was rather quiet as Colonel Tran Hoc stepped from the dressing room.

There were several other men working out during this time between classes. Tran knelt down and slowly sank into deep breathing exercises as he delved within his own being for the concentration he desired.

After this preparation, he got to his feet and began a slow *kata* — the dancelike exercise that simulates fighting an opponent. He moved deliberately and leisurely as he warmed up. Within a few minutes his speed increased until his moves snapped with lightning rapidity, his skill in karate coming to the fore. Various punches and kicks punctuated the drill as he feigned both attack and defense against single and multiple assailants.

Soon Tran's loose flowing uniform was soaked in sweat, and the perspiration flew from his head as he whirled and slashed with feet, hands, knees, and elbows. His yells echoed throughout the near-empty chamber.

Then he stopped.

Tran sank back into a kneeling position and cooled down with the same breathing exercises that had warmed him up to the violent workout.

Tran Hoc, as a police colonel, led a life that offered contacts with individuals from many spheres of the local and foreign population.

He had worked closely with Clayton Andrews of the American Central Intelligence Agency on occasion. In fact, he had led Andrews to a valuable contact prior to the Black Eagles' operation against Camp Three. An ex-French Foreign Legionnaire name Bruno Hosteins had served in the very operational area that Falconi and his men were to penetrate. Through Tran's efforts—and bribes in U.S. currency—Hosteins was persuaded to participate in the operation. Even though he didn't survive, he contributed much to the mission in the way of guidance and scouting activities.

Tran himself was not above taking additional payment for any extracurricular activities in which he participated. While a staunch and sincere anti-Communist—he could never have been paid enough to become a traitor—he had no objection to skipping over certain channels and procedures. Tran would gladly divulge information he had if it would prove beneficial in the struggle against Red encroachment in the south. He reasoned that while he, indeed, received personal benefit, his activities expedited matters in most cases and caused suffering and hurt within subversive ranks.

His second set of respiratory exercises completed, Tran got to his feet and walked across the *dojo* to the punching area. There were two men working out there. One, a rather chubby type, was practicing delivering *jun-geri* kicks to an elongated padded device mounted on the wall. The second was a young man who was much taller than average for an Oriental. Muscular and serious-looking, he methodically drove his fists down into a large vat of sand.

Tran stepped between the two before a small circular target. Wordlessly he alternated *nukite* straight-fingered jabs with *shuto* side-hand slashes, increasing the force of the blows until he had reached the same intensity he had used in the final phases of his *kata*.

After a quarter of an hour the plump man ceases his kicking and picked up a towel lying at his feet to wipe his face. Then he walked away toward the dressing room on the other side of the large room.

Tran looked at his companion. *Ong manh gioi cho?"*

The large, young man continued his rhythmic punching. "Fine, thank you."

"How goes the penetration of Tsing Chai's organization?"

"Quite well, *Dai Ta*. I have been moved inside as a guard on the door to Tsing's office." He was a young police sergeant of Chinese ancestry named Chin.

Tran smiled. "Excellent, *Trung-si* Chin. Do you have access to his desk or living quarters?"

"Not yet, *Dai Ta*," the man answered. "But I am at a position in which I catch many of Tsing Chai's conversations with others."

"Would that include our honorable *Dai Ta* Ngai?" Tran asked.

"Yes. But so far only a few words before they disappear into Tsing's office."

"You must gain entry," Tran emphasized. "And we must have a good case on him. That means, of course, that incriminating documents are of the utmost importance. And I remind you that all of this is outside normal investigation procedures and cases. Discretion is very important until we get some hard evidence on him."

"*Chac-chan,*" Chin acknowledged. "I will proceed accordingly, *Dai Ta.*"

"Excellent! I have slipped some money into the ventilation grill of your locker. You may go now."

"Yes, *Dai Ta,*" Chin said respectfully. "*Chao ong.*"

"*Chao ong.*"

Tran again turned his attention to the *makawara* in front of him. Within moments the room vibrated with the sounds of the blows he administered to it.

Once again Tran threw himself wholly and without reservation into his martial arts workout. His entire being concentrated on the exercise to the extent that his energy flowed like an electrical current to enhance the blows and kicks from his expert fists and hand. The colonel didn't cease his activity until the early afternoon class filed into the *dojo.*

Ngai Quang nodded his thanks to the MP sergeant who had opened the door for him. He stepped into Andrea Thuy's office and smiled a greeting to her.

Andrea stood up and assumed the position of attention. "*Chao ong, Dai Ta* Ngai."

"*Chao co, Trung Úy* Thuy. I trust that Mister Fagin is in.*"

"Yes, *Dai Ta.* He is waiting for you and has asked that you be admitted without delay," Andrea said. "Please follow me."

"*Cam on co,*" Ngai said trailing after the young woman.

Chuck Fagin stood up, smiling, and walked around his desk with his hand extended. "How are you today, Colonel Ngai? Ready for your briefing?"

"Yes, thank you, Mister Fagin," Ngai said. Although the ARVN officer's smile seemed genuine, he had begun to develop an uneasy feeling about the ruddy American that surpassed even his previous feelings during the times of open unfriendliness between them. Ngai couldn't accept the fact that Fagin would cave in with such cheerful abandon to his demands.

"Sit down and make yourself comfortable," Fagin said. He walked to a corner of the office where an art easel sat. He removed the blanket covering it to reveal a map of the northern section of South Vietnam. Picking up a pointer, Fagin indicated a spot just south of the border. "Here's where the Black Eagles are as of their last report."

"And when was this information received, please?" Ngai asked.

"Only two hours previously," Fagin replied.

"Here are copies of the communications log," Andrea said. She handed several pages to the colonel. "They will substantiate what you are about to be told."

"Thank you," Ngai said. He had no doubts the documents were genuine. Even Fagin dared not go against orders directly issued to him from the Central Intelligence Agency's upper echelons. The fact that Clayton Andrews had brought him personally to ARVN headquarters to apologize was convincing evidence of that. "Please continue."

"Our detachment under the command of Major Robert Falconi has established physical contact between themselves and an East European unit made up of Germans," Fagin said.

Andrea interjected. "We have determined that the Caucasians have been wearing American uniforms and committing atrocities that would be attributed to U.S. forces."

"This would be hard to prove," Ngai said.

"Not if we get a prisoner or two," Fagin remarked.

"Do you think this possible?"

"That is exactly what we're working on," Fagin said. "As I stated, our Black Eagles have made contact and are in pursuit of the interlopers who are doing their best to escape beyond their grasp into North Vietnam."

"And you think that Major Falconi will be able to close with them?"

"No doubt," Fagin said.

Andrea again joined the conversation. "Every effort is directed toward this end, *Dai Ta*. The Black Eagles, who are in much better physical condition for jungle fighting than the Europeans expect to literally run them down."

"And when Robert Falconi says he's going to drive 'em into the ground, he'll do just that," Fagin remarked.

"No doubt," Ngai said. "May I please see their exact location again? I would like to note the grid coordinates for the report I must prepare for my superiors."

"Of course," Fagin said. "In fact, Lieutenant Thuy has prepared a complete statement for you which includes that information. Right, Lieutenant?"

"Yes," Andrea said. "I shall give it to you on your way out, *Dai Ta*."

"Thank you," Ngai said. He knew that Fagin was up to something. Although forced to hand over information by his superiors, there was always the possibility that the CIA man would bypass normal channels to seek out information he needed—or get certain things done.

"To continue," Fagin said. "Right now Falconi is planning on intercepting the East Germans before they can reach the sanctuary of North Vietnam. Once that is done, he will engage them in combat and, hopefully, get the prisoners and bodies he will need to substantiate our allegations of Communist Europeans committing war crimes within operational areas in South Vietnam. His exfiltration will be handled by choppers from the landing zone"—he pointed to the map—"right here. From there they will fly to Danang. After changing over to high performance aircraft, the detachment—with prisoners—will continue to Tan Son Nhut and both our authorities and those of your country will begin an exhaustive interrogation and investigation of the prisoners until our case is made and we can present it to the world."

"And how is the latter to be accomplished?" Ngai asked.

Fagin shrugged. "I really don't know, Colonel. Nobody has briefed me on that since I won't be concerned with that phase of the situation. I presume they'll go to the United Nations."

"Well," Colonel Ngai said. "That isn't our worry anyway. People who are far above our little positions in this struggle will take care of that."

"I suppose," Fagin said. "Shall we continue with the briefing?"

"Please!"

Both Fagin and Andrea brought the ARVN officer up to date on every aspect of the latest activities concerning Falconi and his men. As per orders received from higher echelons, they left out nothing. Even the make up of the two fire teams was included. The pair purposely exaggerated and expanded the report until it became dry and boring.

But, whatever happened in the long run, Fagin wanted his ass covered. If Ngai turned out to be okay—which he doubted—then his cooperation would be correctly and duly noted. If the colonel was finally shown up as an enemy agent, then that would become apparent from certain actions taken by the other side. Ngai was now in receipt of information that the enemy could never know without his passing it on to them.

Ngai stood up. "Thank you so much, Mister Fagin. Our new friendship is becoming a warm part of my life."

"And for me too, Colonel," Fagin said smiling. "Good day, sir."

"Good day." Ngai turned to Andrea. *"Chao co, Trung Úy Thuy."*

Again Andrea snapped to attention. *"Chao ong, Dai Ta Ngai."*

After Ngai left, Fagin was silent for several long moments. When he finally spoke, his voice was subdued and almost sad.

"Why do I keep getting the feeling that I've just murdered Robert Falconi and company?"

Sergeant Chin, in his undercover role as a bodyguard for Tsing Chai, walked through the empty gambling parlor. He knew this was the hour that the Chinese gaming master liked to visit his favorite restaurant. The only other security in the vicinity would be the two guards on the outside door. Chin, arriving for duty a couple of hours early, explained to the doormen that he'd left his wallet behind that morning after his shift was over.

In order to cover himself, Chin had purposely put his billfold, filled with piastres, on a table in the room used by the security men during their breaks. It spoke for their honesty that it was still there when he returned.

He stuck the wallet in his pocket and walked out of the lounge down the hall past Tsing's office. He continued to the curtain that led to the gaming area and stepped. A quick glance showed the room to be empty. He turned back toward Tsing's office, pulling the special skeleton key from his pocket.

Within forty-five seconds the door popped open and he stopped inside. Without wasting any precious time, Chin hurried to the desk. The top drawer was unlocked. A quick search showed nothing but miscellaneous business papers. The other various compartments were the same.

Chin noted the door leading to another room. He carefully approached it and pressed his ear against the paneling to see if he could distinguish anyone on the other side.

Nothing.

The young police sergeant tried the knob and it wouldn't budge. He pulled out his ring of keys and picked a likely one. He deftly inserted it and worked the instrument back and forth until the latch gave and the portal, surprisingly thick and heavy, swung open.

Chin stepped through in time to catch a vicious *seiken* jab from the guard on the other side.

CHAPTER SIXTEEN

It was lucky for the Black Eagles that it was Popeye Jenkins who first spotted the East Germans.

If Dinky Dow, leading their small column, had caught sight of the Europeans, he would have lost all sense of reason and charged ahead. The men behind him, used to Archie Dobbs's efficiency on the point, would have followed the crazy little fellow straight into an unmitigated disaster.

Popeye, now fully recovered from the effects of the muted grenade blast, was responsible for security on the right flank. The navy SEAL visually swept the vegetation on that side with quick gazes. His keen eyes were alert for any foreign objects in the trees and brush. He had learned long ago that fixed staring did not aid a man when he was looking for the unknown. It only served to momentarily blur his vision from time to time.

The German's face, though streaked with dark green camouflage paint, had popped out at the navy SEAL like a bare ass at a Baptist convention. Jenkins took a quick, sight picture and pulled the trigger. The man's features exploded in a spray of red at the exact moment Popeye yelled out the alarm.

"Ambush! Right flank!"

As per Falconi's Standing Operational Procedure, the Black Eagles immediately whirled and charged in that direction, their M-16s barking in the density of the jungle. Up ahead, Dinky Dow spun on his heel and rushed back to join the action, angling off into the thick bushes.

The little Vietnamese stumbled across the Germans' forward position. He fired once and missed. His second shot took out one of the Red riflemen, but the Commie's buddy was quick. He took three steps and smashed his rifle butt into Dinky Dow's chest.

"Klein Bastard du!"

Dinky Dow went over on his back and continued to roll until he reached a sitting position. With his breath knocked out and his head swirling, he raised the M-16 he had only barely managed to hang on to. He fired almost blindly at the hulking figure above him and was rewarded with the sight of the man staggering backward to trip over his friend. Pure instinct guided the little ARVN officer now. He struggled to his feet and shot at the two indistinct men to his front before he fell down again. He gasped hoarsely as his breath slowly returned.

Back in Bravo Team, Malpractice McCorckel ordered Chun Kim and Calvin Culpepper to begin the enveloping part of the operation.

Calvin, firing rapidly but steadily, advanced into the trees with his Korean cohort slightly behind him. He could see no targets, so he aimed low using his fusillades to sweep the area in front of him while Kim pumped 40-millimeter grenades through the lighter limbs above them. The projectiles cut through these to explode far-ther away, sending metal fragments slicing groundward in a deadly, metal rain.

Malpractice backed them both up by hosing the area with full automatic fire as the small team sought to cut off the ambushers in a maneuver designed to catch the enemy in a small pincers formation.

Top Gordon scurried forward behind the intrepid trio of Archie Dobbs, Popeye Jenkins, and Sparks Jackson as they penetrated the enemy position. The three sounded like a small independent war of their own as their combined firepower spat angry, buzzing bullets through the undergrowth.

Archie, slightly ahead of the others, leaped over the body of one German. The man, a perfect Teutonic spec-imen with blond hair and blue eyes, sprawled in gap-mouthed death. The Red's American weapon lay a couple of feet away where it had fallen when the two bul-lets that killed its owner struck their mortal blows.

Top had to slow his men down a bit to prevent them from getting in too far until the Bravos had finished their maneuvering. It was bad enough to have enemy fire cut you down without running the risk of charging into your own men's explosive volleys.

Falconi, figuring that Dinky Dow had involved him-self away from the others, rushed forward to catch up with Top. "Give the Bravos a chance to do their thing!" he cautioned him as he caught up with the detachment sergeant.

"I'm trying to, Skipper," Top said over his shoulder as he advanced. "But the ambushers are pulling back as fast as we rush 'em."

"Keep the pressure on," Falconi cautioned him. "But

stay coordinated with Malpractice."

"I'll try," Top promised. "But if I slow down, those fucking Krauts are going to give us the slip again."

Falconi indicated his understanding with a nod of his head as the small battle continued to roar through the jungle's thick stands of trees.

Sergeant Chin staggered back into Tsing Chai's office as the man who had delivered the punch followed up with a slashing crescent kick.

Chin went under his assailant's foot and grabbed it, twisting violently. The man, who was Tsing Chai's radio operator, screamed in agony as the tibia in his ankle gave way with a loud crack. Chin's *seiken* punch to the jaw snapped his head back, and the radioman dropped to the thick carpet on the floor like a sack of wet sand.

But the door leading from the hallway burst open and three more of Tsing's bodyguards charged into the room.

The leading man, a burly Sumo wrestler type, was a huge mountain of muscle and flesh. He glared at Chin. *"Cai nay la cai gi?"* the fat man asked.

Chin pointed to the fallen radioman. "He attacked me."

The injured fighter weakly raised his head. "The bastard was—prowling in here—and tried—to get into—the—radio room."

The fat guard reached inside his suit coat to draw his pistol but Chin was too quick for him. He smashed down on his forearm with the knife edge of his hand in a *shuto* chop.

The second man, a very short copy of the larger guard, managed to pull his own Colt automatic from his

176

shoulder holster.

"No!" Fat Guard exclaimed. "We'll take him alive!"

"Chac-chan," Short Guard agreed. He immediately charged Chin.

The police sergeant met the second attacker's impetuous assault with a beautifully executed *sokotu-geri* side kick. Due to the man's diminutive height, Chin didn't have to raise his leg too high to make contact and knock him crashing on top of the radio operator.

The third attacker, a skinny, more agile man had begun his own charge a split second after his less fortunate buddy. His roundhouse clenched-fist *furi-zuki* punch missed its original target of Chin's ear, but it did land with bruising force on the young sergeant's right deltoid muscle. The blow spun Chin completely around so that his back was to his assailant.

He found himself once again facing Fat Guard.

Chin, knowing the skinny man behind him was slightly off balance, ignored him and launched himself at the heavier opponent. His first blow was made with the heel of his hand directly to the point of the chin, while his left knuckle, protruding from his fist, was stabbed into the solar plexus. Fat Guard only grunted, but he stumbled back through the open door.

Chin turned to meet Skinny Guard's next effort with a *uchi-uke* forearm block; then he whirled on his heel until his back was to the man. He drove his elbow into his opponent's midsection with explosive force. A loud grunt announced violent contact and Skinny rolled to the floor.

Fat Guard, having made a sudden recovery from Chin's attack and bellowing in rage charged back through the door. Chin waited until the last minute, then rolled out of the way letting Fat Guard's momentum carry him far enough forward to stumble over Skinny Guard who was struggling to his feet.

Both went down together.

Short Guard, meanwhile having freed himself from being entangled with the injured radioman, came back into the fray with a vengeance. He faked a charge and pulled back to dodge Chin's panther punch. He feinted toward the policeman's head and kicked out toward his knee.

The foot, while missing the more vulnerable part of Chin's leg, did manage to smash into the back of his calf. Chin yelled out in pain and flung a blindly instinctive horizontal *shuto* that smashed Short Guard's nose into a pulverized mesh of cartilage and bloody mucus. Chin then drove the heel of his other hand into the mess between his assailant's eyes. Shards of bone from the broken nose broke loose under the force of the blow and penetrated upward into Short Guard's brain.

He died while still on his feet.

His legs, receiving crazy, uncoordinated messages from his expiring brain, jerked around in a purely instinctive effort to escape the danger. But his knees gave out and Short Guard, blood gushing from his destroyed nose, collapsed into a twisted heap.

Fat Guard and Skinny Guard charged together now.

Chin faked a move toward Fat Guard, then rolled to his left and caught Skinny Guard's right arm. He pulled toward him, then rolled around dragging his opponent with him. He suddenly ducked his shoulders and pulled down hard on Skinny Guard's arm.

The man's feet flew up and he went over Chin's head. His flying body collided with Fat Guard's, but the larger man caught his partner and hurled him violently over his own shoulder to continue the maneuver Chin had started.

Skinny Guard crashed into the wall face-first, leaving a smear of blood as he slowly slid to his knees. Then he toppled backward with a loud groan.

Fat Guard caught Chin off balance with his counter. He slammed a closed fist up in a bolo-like *uraken* punch that caught the police sergeant square in the face. Chin unwittingly came to a full-standing position just in time to catch a straight *nukite* jab in his throat.

Blood was spurting from the sergeant's nose and mouth as Fat Guard, his huge bulk vibrating with the effort, began the first of several hammerlike bottom-of-the-fist blows that slammed like pile drivers onto Chin's head and shoulders.

"Those bastards fight like *Löwen!*" Kamerad Leutnant Willi Feldhaus said in reluctant admiration.

Stahler lit a cigarette and expelled the smoke before speaking. "You didn't expect to be sent all the way out here from Europe to fight a bunch of *Miesen,* did you?"

"No, *Kamerad Hauptmann,* I most certainly did not anticipate mice," Feldhaus assured him. "But I didn't expect to encounter lions either."

The two officers had taken refuge behind a thick stand of bamboo that lay between them and the battle. The sound of the fighting was more sporadic now. At various times it would die off completely for several moments, then slowly build up to a peak before stopping.

"How is our maneuvering going?" Stahler asked his subordinate.

"That is the reason I've reported back to you, *Kamerad Hauptmann,*" Feldhaus said. "I'm losing contact with the men on the left. The fighting grew heavier on the other flank so I went over there to pull them back."

"*Sehr gut,* Willi!" Stahler said with approval. "If one side of our line falls, then we'll be enveloped and eventually surrounded instead of leading Falconi and his men in the direction we desire." He took out his field radio and contacted the sergeant in charge of the left section. After ordering the NCO to move his men back and cover the faltering right, he turned back to Feldhaus. "Go back and help out on the left, Willi. They haven't taken as many casualties and the men there may become a bit more aggressive than is good for them or our tactics in this instance. The withdrawal must continue with Falconi closely following, *äusterlich versagen* — without fail!"

Feldhaus executed a quick, butt sharp salute. "*Jawohl, Kamerad Hauptmann!*"

Then he rushed back to his duties.

Stahler watched his subordinate leave, then calmly dropped his cigarette but to the ground and stepped on it. Promotion in the East German forces was slow, but with a coup like the one he was about to score against the Black Eagles, he could well be wearing colonel's epaulettes a good five years before his time.

Sweat streamed down Falconi's face as he hit the transmit button on the Prick-Six. "Alpha this is Falcon. Over."

Top Gordon's voice, distorted but recognizable, came back through the ear piece. "This is Alpha. Over."

"What the fuck's going on? I can hardly keep up with

you guys. Over."

Top, moving rapidly through the jungle, had trouble speaking. "We got 'em—on the run—trying to corner—the bastards before—they get completely—away and out of touch—over."

"Roger," Falconi acknowledged. "Have you seen Dinky Dow? Over."

Before Top could answer, Malpractice McCorckel, who had been monitoring the conversation over his own radio, cut in. "This is Bravo. He's with us, Falcon. Caught a butt stroke in the chest and is bruised but still game. Over."

Falconi, who could picture the extremely angry little guy, grinned to himself. "Roger, Bravo. Let him stay with you. I'll be catching up immediately. Out."

The Black Eagles' commander, feeling they were about to close in on the elusive Germans, slung the radio across his shoulder and once again turned his attention to his M-16 rifle. The Reds would have to peter out quickly now. The battle had evidently turned into a fox hunt with the quarry being literally run into the ground.

Falconi gritted his teeth and increased his pace even more.

Other radio communications had been zipping along their own wave lengths not too far away.

General Vang, commanding the entrenched 327th Infantry Battalion of the North Vietnamese Army, grinned widely as he handed the transmitter/receiver back to his radio operator.

His adjutant noted the general's expression. The captain sensed exciting or good news. "What word have you received, Comrade *Thiêú Tuóng?*"

"Our plans are working perfectly," Vang answered, rubbing his hands together in anticipation. "The East Germans are executing their part of the operation with absolute perfection."

The adjutant now smiled too. "Then it is only a matter of a short time before Falconi and his Black Eagles fall into our trap."

"That is what the situation has evolved into now," Vang agreed. "The question is no longer *if* we score a victory, but *when*."

"I have studied the map of this area most carefully, Comrade *Thiếú Tướng*," the adjutant said. "And I can perceive no way for the Black Eagles to even be able to run away."

"Indeed!" Vang exclaimed. "And the slaughter on the Song Bo will be completely and undeniably avenged!"

CHAPTER SEVENTEEN

The two policeman cautiously pushed their way through the crowd that had assembled at the alley entrance.

This was the infamous Cholon District of Saigon; thus, the two lawmen were alert and prepared for any danger or treachery. It was in this section of the sprawling city that dope dealers, pimps, and other criminals existed hand in hand with secret agents of the Viet Cong. In the Cholon, a working policeman or soldier could never be sure he wouldn't be murdered because of political motivations or his work of enforcing the law.

The two uniformed officers kept a nervous eye on the people around them as they worked their way through the milling group. A quick knife thrust would be a distinct possibility in a situation like this.

They finally reached the edge of the crowd to see what had attracted the group's curiosity. The body of a naked man was sprawled out on a garbage heap, his corpse in the first stages of decay in the hot tropical sun that slashed between the buildings bordering the narrow thoroughfare.

There was no denying the dead man had met his end through violent means. His face was so badly beaten it had been difficult to determine his Oriental race. There were bruises and burns over the body's torso, along with deep gashes and wide areas of raw, scraped skin.

A most unpleasant death.

The first officer gazed down at the cadaver without much interest. "Looks like some narcotics peddler had a falling out with his friends," he quickly surmised.

"It must have been a very serious disagreement. They took their time in killing the poor bastard. No doubt he did something that upset them," mused his partner. He looked down at the victim. "Seems rather large, doesn't he?"

"Yes," the other agreed. "When I first sighted him through the mob here, I thought he might be an American."

"Muscular fellow," the first policemen said. "Maybe he worked as some big shot's personal bodyguard."

"Mmmm, yes." The second leaned over the man and made a quick, visual inspection. "Well nourished, heavily built — those hands are tough and callused —"

"A martial artist, no doubt," his companion added.

"Indeed. Seems clean — the fingernails are clipped short and his hair is neatly trimmed."

The people gathered in the alley had edged forward a bit, so the other policeman pushed them back. "Don't crowd us. You've all had a good look."

The first officer turned to the onlookers. "Does anyone know this man?"

As usual there was a talkative individual who, despite the local dislike and distrust of the police, was happy to speak out and gain the center of his neighbors' attention. "I don't know his name, but I've seen him around here before."

One of the policemen turned to the man who owned a small fruit stand. "Where did you notice him?"

"Walking around the neighborhood," the street peddler answered. "He was always well dressed in a western-style suit. I think he worked at one of the gambling places—but I can't recall which one."

"Wait!" The other policeman, who had been giving the body a close examination, motioned to his partner. "I know who he is now. It took me a few moments, but I have absolutely no doubts about it."

"I don't know how you can tell the way his face has been battered in."

"It took me a few minutes," the policeman said. "But I'm sure now—it's Sergeant Chin."

"Do you mean from Colonel Tran's staff?"

"The same."

The policeman shook his head. "Hell is going to break loose in the Cholon before this is over."

Falconi, with Top Gordon and Malpractice McCorckel serving as subordinate leaders, continued to press the Black Eagles Detachment in its relentless pursuit of the East Germans who had been masquerading as Americans.

It was a frustrating undertaking.

No sooner would the Black Eagles make contact and launch into what seemed would be an all-out battle, than the Reds would pull back and run like hell until they decided to stop and fight one more time.

Then, after a brief but thundering encounter, the cat-

and-mouse game would begin one more time.

The biggest problem for Falconi was to maintain control of his men. They seemed to scatter more with each engagement. At one point Malpractice managed to get completely out of range of the Prick-Six radios they used for communications. There were a few tense moments until the Bravos—the fire team he was leading—managed to edge back within broadcast distance.

Master Sergeant Top Gordon, now fighting in his second war, had begun to have misgivings about the entire operation. After the fifth brief encounter of the day, he requested a meeting between Falcon, Malpractice, and himself.

When the trio gathered together within a hastily thrown-up perimeter, Falconi looked pointedly at the detachment's senior NCO. "You got something on your mind, Top?"

"Yeah, Skipper. I think we'd better calm down a little here and run this situation through a careful discussion."

Falconi glanced at Malpractice. Although a medic, the sergeant was a seasoned combat leader with plenty of know-how on what he was doing—no matter if it was the killing or healing side of soldiering. The major asked, "What's your opinion, Malpractice?"

"We seem to be kickin' ass—as Dinky Dow would say—so why let up now?"

"Something fishy is going on," Top countered. "I've fought both against and in withdrawals and delaying actions. There's a decidedly unkosher air about this one."

Falconi shrugged. "It appears nearly classical to me. They run like hell, then turn and fight. Then run some more. Seems like an operation right out of the textbook to me."

"Except for one thing," Top said. "These guys aren't part of a larger force. They're not protecting anybody. So they should be able to haul ass through this jungle by splitting up into small teams. Hell, if they did that, we'd never get any of 'em. It's like they really don't want to break contact."

"Keep one important thing in mind, Top," Malpractice said. "Them guys ain't the experts in this line o'work that we are. They're pretty fresh outta the meadows and forests of Europe where there's plenty of towns and a denser population. They're used to having armor support, artillery, and other goodies."

"What're you trying to say, Malpractice?" Falconi asked.

"I don't think the dumb bastards know what they're doin," Malpractice said. "Their leader is fuckin' up like a T-5 parachute and we'll wrap him and his squareheads up any time now."

"I'm not so sure," Top insisted. "I keep getting this gut feeling that I'm being led along like I had a ring through my nose. And I don't like it."

"What do you suggest then?" Falconi asked.

"I think we ought to be more cautious," Top advised. "Maybe make some probes and recons with two-man teams to really determine what the situation is."

"Caution means slowing down," Falconi reminded him. "That's something we can't afford. Remember the North Vietnamese border isn't too far away."

Top shrugged. "We've done all our work behind the lines anyhow."

"He's right there, Skipper," Malpractice said.

"Yeah," Falconi agreed. "But we weren't worried

187

about having to get prisoners and drag them all the way back to safer territory."

"I don't know, Skipper," Malpractice contradicted. "That's what we did on the Song Bo."

"We already had the prisoners," Falconi said. "In fact we practically started out the operation with the bastards in our custody. In this instance, we have to chase those Krauts clear to Hanoi—maybe—grab a couple, then head south with a howling mob on our heels."

Top shook his head. "I just don't know."

"Hey, Top," Falconi said. "Don't think I've got the idea that you're all wet. Arguing helps me make decisions."

"Me too, Skipper. And I'm arguing that the sons-of-bitches want us to chase after 'em for some reason or another."

"Why would they?" Malpractice asked.

"To get us over on the other side of that fucking border," Top said. "God only knows what's waiting for us up there. You can make book that they've undoubtedly informed their own people up there that they've been forced to bug outta their Operational Area."

"The more reason to grab a couple as quickly as possible," Falconi said. "Then we can be the ones shagging ass out of the OA."

"I say we press on," Malpractice said.

"And I say we don't," Top said.

Falconi fell into a deep silence, weighing the facts and opinions presented to him by the two seasoned noncommissioned officers. The situation had reached the one point of decision making he hated the most. No matter what he decided, he was damned if he did, and damned if he didn't in either fighting on or showing more caution.

A few moments later he spoke.

"We have orders to take prisoners and evacuate them to our own people. We have to do that. No ifs, ands, or buts. So we press on like before."

Top, ever the soldier, accepted his commander's decision calmly. "Right, Skipper. Want me and my boys to lead out?"

"Go to it, top. And remember—"

"I know," Top said interrupting with a wide grin. "Nobody said this fucking job was going to be easy."

"Right! Let's go!"

The war was on again.

Marcel Tailleur leaned across the counter of his café and idly thumbed through a two-month-old copy of *Paris Match*.

He was a dark, balding man with heavy unshaven jowls and a protruding belly. Fat and slow, he was languidly smoking a cheap stogie. He pulled the smelly cigar from his thick lips to belch loudly. Then, unconcerned about the ashes that periodically cascaded from the cheap cigar to flutter down over his shirt, he replaced it between his yellowed teeth.

The customers of Chez Marcel had increased lately, but certainly not from any improvement in the cuisine or *boisson* offered by the trashy establishment. Marcel Tailleur's only real competition in the Quartier des Colons had been a bar and café called La Coloniale.

That particular bistro had been run by an ex-Foreign Legionnaire named Bruno Hosteins. Hosteins, while certainly no gourmet or *connaisseur des vins* at least ran his business with a good deal of cleanliness and a genuine attempt to present food and drink of good quality to his clientele.

But Bruno Hosteins was gone now.

Word was that he'd been caught in a terrorist bomb blast in another part of the city. Blown to pieces the size of grains of sand, the German who had spent fifteen years of his life serving France had been sent to his resting place with a simple memorial ceremony. The well-attended event had been held in the Quartier des Colons small Catholic Church.

There evidently hadn't been enough of him left to put into a coffin. His mourners were unaware he had died on a clandestine raid into North Vietnam. All they knew was that Hosteins was gone forever, and from that day forward they would be forced to partake of Marcel Tailleur's rather shabby fare.

"Marcel." One of the customers at the bar spoke to him.

"Oui?"

"A customer has sat down at one of your outside tables," the man said.

Marcel turned his attention back to the magazine. "So? You are worried if he's hungry or thirsty?"

"Mais non!" the man answered. He held up his glass of red wine. "I just want to see some other poor *type* have to suffer one of your glasses of *vin* besides myself."

Marcel spat. *"Mangez merde."*

"Eat shit yourself," the customer snapped. "You'd better see to the stranger's wants. He is usually joined at his table by Colonel Tran."

"Quel souci," Marcel complained. He reluctantly left his reading material and wandered out to the table. He looked down at the man sitting there. *"Oui, monsieur?"*

"A glass of red wine," Chuck Fagin said.

Marcel started to leave when Colonel Tran strode up and sat down. The café owner nodded to the policeman. *"Désirez-vous quelque chose, monsieur le colonel?"*

Tran shook his head. "No," he said pointedly. Then he sat down. He waited the few minutes it took Marcel to go inside and return with the wine, then leave again before he spoke. His voice betrayed his anger. "Chin is dead."

Fagin raised his eyebrows quizzically. "Who is Chin?"

"He was the man I had working inside Tsing Chai's on the Ngai case for you," Tran said.

"I'm sorry to hear it."

Tran was a highly-trained martial artist. As such he had gone past the point of uncontrolled outbursts of temper. Instead his anger was cold, calculated—and deadly. "I will require no further payment from you involving this investigation, Mister Fagin."

"You're dropping the case?"

"Of course not," Tran said. "When Tsing killed Chin—or had him killed—he declared war on me personally. Nobody eliminates any of my men and gets away with it."

"I understand. But, on the other hand, Tsing Chai was unaware that Chin was one of your men."

"It makes no difference in the slightest!" Tran said.

"That's a new twist for me," Fagin said. "In America, such revenge by the police is nearly impossible."

"My hands are not tied by constitutional law," Tran said. "And I do not intend to let this matter drop."

"Are you sure that Tsing is responsible?"

"Chin's body was found in an alley in the Cholon district," Tran explained. "He'd been badly beaten and tortured. The autopsy revealed he'd died from the torments inflicted on him."

"I'm sorry to hear about your man," Fagin said. "But please allow me a cold calculated question at this point. Do you think he talked?"

"No," Tran answered. "For several reasons I believe he maintained his silence. If he'd broken down they would have killed him with a shot to the head at the end of the torture session. Instead he died under interrogation. I also don't think he revealed any information because he was a *karateka*—and able to withstand the pain inflicted on him."

"Are you sure?"

"The types of wounds he suffered would not cause him to lose control despite the agony inflicted," Tran explained. "Chin would have withdrawn into himself and blocked out all outside interferences about him. He had spent years perfecting his meditation and concentration. Chin's control over his mind and body was nearly total."

"Again, permit me to seem unconcerned and cold," Fagin said. "But are you putting another man in his place?"

"As quickly as possible," Tran said. "Chin had a younger brother who now seeks vengeance for his brother's murder. Corporal Chin Han is now on the case."

"I am glad to hear that," Fagin said. "But do you think it wise for a man as obviously emotionally involved as Chin's brother to put on the case."

"The young man is also a *karateka*," Tran explained. "He will be able to control himself perfectly in order to attain his most cherished goal of revenging his kinsman."

"I admire those traits very much," Fagin said sincerely. "And please allow me to express my sorrow at the loss of Sergeant Chin."

Tran stood up. "I hope we can wrap up this case before any real harm comes to your Major Falconi and his men."

Fagin took a sip of the bad wine, then set it down again. "I'm afraid it's too late to save Falconi from whatever danger he may be in. If he gets out of this mess with Ngai knowing every step he takes, it'll be by the skin of his ass."

"In a war men must die," Tran said.

CHAPTER EIGHTEEN

"Keep it moving! Don't lag!"

Top Gordon's voice directed both his own Alpha Fire Team and Malpractice McCorkel's Bravos as they swept through the jungle in a near classic As-Skirmishers formation.

Short, harmless fire fights had marked most of the early afternoon's activities.

They had not even seen the East Germans except for some occasional brief glances, and there had been no bodies left for them to examine.

Dinky Dow and Archie Dobbs, who had been sent forward as a reconnaissance team, returned to the detachment's position. They threaded their way through the Black Eagles to find their commanding officer.

Falconi greeted them with only a tired nod. "What's up there?"

"Nothing, Skipper," Archie said. "We can just see faint trails where the bastards skipped through. They must be running as fast as their fat little Kraut legs will carry 'em."

"We run too! Dinky Dow insisted. "Kill the mother-fuckers!"

"Goddamn it!" Falconi swore. "The bastards are going to get away from us as sure as shit stinks."

"We'd better press on," Archie advised him.

"You're right there," Falconi said. "Get back on line and tell Top to speed things up. I think they're drawing out of our clutches."

"Right, Skipper," Archie said. He turned and trotted back to join the skirmishers with Dinky Dow on his heels.

Stahler breathed hard as he pressed on through the clinging thickness of the vegetation. The survivors of his East German detachment followed as young Leutnant Willi Feldhaus and the NCOs urged them on.

At this point in the overall plan they had to avoid contact with the Black Eagles at all costs. Falconi and his men had literally worn them down. Exhausted, nearly demoralized, and suffering from both hunger and thirst, the European Communists were at the end of their tether.

Stahler froze at the sound of the high-pitched voice ahead of him.

Ong quc-tich gì?"

The meaning of the words were lost on him, but he knew the sound from having had it drilled into his memory. He had also memorized the proper password.

"Toy la nguò dúrc," Stahler said. Then he repeated the phrase he had learned phonetically. *"Toy la nguò dúrc."*

Within moments another voice spoke, this one in English. "Welcome to the area of the 327the Infantry

Battalion, Captain Stahler."

Stahler continued through the brush until he met up with a crisp, young NVA captain. The officer smiled and saluted. "I am General Vang's adjutant. Please forgive me, as I must speak in English because of my regrettable ignorance of the German language."

Stahler, despite a burning fatigue, was able to display his own brand of diplomacy. "And I must beg your pardon because I cannot speak Vietnamese," he said, returning the other's salute. "I am at your service. My troops are to my immediate rear and rapidly approaching."

"What about the Black Eagle Detachment?" the adjutant asked.

"They are right on our heels."

The adjutant's smile widened. "Then they are walking straight into our trap."

"Yes," Stahler agreed. "Our tactics of keeping just ahead of them forced their commander to hurry his men along in a manner not quite suited to the tactical situation. I must admit a grudging admiration for his courage in the circumstances. He is most certainly not a timid man."

"Timid or brave," the adjutant said. "He will be within striking distance of the entire 327th Infantry Battalion in a very short time."

Dinky Dow was angry.

It seemed no matter how fast he moved his short legs he couldn't get himself back within sight of the Germans.

He'd felt a great sense of relief when Falconi had taken him from command of Alpha Fire Team. Dinky

Dow knew he was a lousy combat leader. His hatred of the Viet Cong and the NVA was so fierce, encompassing his every conscious thought and instinct, that he could no control himself during fighting. Now, with the rest of the Black Eagles part of a skirmish formation, the little Vietnamese officer had pressed ahead on his own.

Then he finally caught sight of the enemy.

But it wasn't one of the Europeans. The man Dinky Dow spotted wore the pith helmet of the NVA. The red star on the front even showed through the camouflage the soldier had placed in the netting on it.

Dinky Dow gasped in rage. He fired his M-16 from the hip and shrieked in joy as the NVA's helmet popped off his head at the impact of the slugs on his body.

But the jungle in front of Dinky Dow exploded and dozens of rounds slammed into his slight frame, tossing him back into the brush two meters to the rear.

There was no pain. Only a numbness and even a certain peacefulness crept into his fading consciousness. Dinky Dow tried to move, but the best he could do was to raise one hand. He noted that three fingers had been shot off it and that blood flowed from the stumps in rivulets down to his elbow. Suddenly he wished he'd done a better job in leading the Alphas for Falconi.

He should have given more attention to the mission's purpose instead of simply wanting to kill the enemy.

He should have taken the time to check out the other guys' ammo and supplies, and things would have gone smoother.

He should have been more cautious during the previous few moments. It was obvious that a large, unexpected enemy force was lying in ambush.

He should have —

Dinky Dow sighed loudly, then took a deep breath. It was his last.

The heavy bursts of gunfire grew and intermingled until a single, relentless roar enveloped the area.

General Vang Ngoc smiled in satisfaction at the sound. He leaned toward Captain Rolf Stahler. "You and your men did an excellent job in leading Falconi and his bandits to us."

Stahler lit a cigarette. He was in Vang's hastily constructed headquarters bunker with the NVA general. "Are you sure you can manage to get Falconi as a prisoner? That amount of shooting may well end up killing him and all his men."

"My orders are to destroy the Black Eagles," Vang reminded him.

"And mine are to see that Falconi is a prisoner," Stahler insisted. "Comrade Colonel Krashchenko has personally charged me with the task."

"I am in command of the 327th," Vang said. "And in that role I shall see that my men continue pressing their attack."

"You'll kill Falconi for sure!" Stahler yelled over the gunfire. "Nothing can live in that hell you've created out there!"

Vang spat. "Nothing is supposed to, Comrade Captain."

Twigs flew through the air as Archie Dobbs, crawling backward on his stomach, squirmed to seek more cover. The buzzing of bullets overhead was continuous and the sounds of the small projectiles slapping into trees punctuated the reports of the weapons firing them.

Sparks Jackson reached out and patted Archie's leg. The navy SEAL motioned him to draw closer. "We got to find Top."

"Who the fuck's shooting at us?" Archie asked.

"Gotta be NVA," Sparks said. "Them Krautheads led us right to 'em."

The two continued to scramble to the rear until they spotted the detachment sergeant. Top signaled them to join him. The deadly curtain of fire just above their heads was invisible. But the pair were aware of its presence as they crawled over.

"The bastards have us pinned down," Top explained to them. "I just talked to the Skipper. He's rounding up Malpractice and the Bravos. As soon as we're all together, we'll try to bug outta here."

"There's gotta be several comp'nies up ahead, Top," Archie said. "And this firepower's something else!"

"As long as they keep shooting we're okay," Top said. "When they stop and come after us is when the shit's really going to hit the fan."

Falconi, with Malpractice, Chun Kim, and Calvin Culpepper behind him, hurried up to join them on his hands and knees. "Any casualties?" the commander asked.

"Yeah," Archie said as the hell above their heads continued. "Dinky Dow caught it right off the bat. I spotted him go down."

"What're his chances?"

Archie shook his head. "He got hit twelve or fifteen times, Skipper."

"The little fucker!" Falconi exclaimed sadly and angrily. He looked over at Top Gordon. "I should've listened to you."

"Yeah," Malpractice added.

"Screw it," Top said. "We're gonna get hit and hit hard in a few minutes. That's what we got to worry about."

"Right," Falconi agreed. "This is as good a spot to defend as any. We can't get up and run anyhow. We'll hang loose and see what direction they'll be coming at us from."

"It'll be from the front, Skipper," Top said. "There's so many of the bastards that they got no reason to try and be fancy with us. They'll charge us head on."

"Okay, Top. Let's get ready for 'em," Falconi said.

The battalion headquarters radio operator turned from his set and spoke excitedly to Vang. "The field commanders have all reported in, Comrade *Thiêú Tu'o'ng*. The imperialists are no longer advancing and have been down."

Vang buckled his pistol belt around his slender waist and slipped his helmet on. He looked at Stahler sitting on the other side of the bunker. "Now we will destroy Falconi and his bandits!" He turned to the young commo man, his eyes alight with furious excitement. "Order the battalion to advance."

Stahler leaped up from where he'd been sitting and cross the sandbagged room. He grabbed Vang's shoulder. "You must not kill Falconi!"

"I will kill all of them!" Vang shrieked in rage at the foreigner who dared to argue with him. "They must all die—everyone!"

Top Gordon, on the extreme left flank of their line, had first contact with the attacking NVA. When he saw how closely packed they were, he flipped his M-16 over

201

to full automatic. The weapon danced as the bullets spurted out in groups of five or six to slash into the packed enemy. The young Reds collapsed in heaps under the onslaught.

On the other side of the line, with only Calvin Culpepper to his right, Chun Kim the Korean marine pumped the final grenades out of the M-79 into the horde of uniforms that had materialized in front of him in the jungle. The front two ranks were blown onto their backs, but their friends behind pressed over their cadavers toward his position.

Calvin took quick, single shots. Each round dropped one of the screaming Reds. Kim abandoned the now useless M-79 and turned to his own M-16. Together he and Calvin held that lone right flank as the enemy dead stretched toward them in an ever-growing carpet, the living pressing forward until they fell when struck by the volleys of the two Black Eagles.

Popeye Jenkins had taken a position behind a thick tree. Despite the enemy bullets gouging the bark around his head, he never flinched. He fired methodically and effectively at the many targets of opportunity ahead of him. A trio of NVA, determined to get him, had managed to crawl unseen through the thick brush to a point only ten feet in front of his position.

They suddenly leaped up and charged the SEAL.

Popeye swung his muzzle left and sent a slug into the chest of the first man. The young Communist sat down hard as the bullet knocked him backward. Without wasting a beat, Popeye took the middle one out with a shot that split the top of the Red's head open. A small, bloody volcano erupted when the bullet exited the skull.

The third man, however, reached the sailor and

charged into him, shrieking with rage. The two collided and rolled over into the brush. Popeye quickly gained the upper hand. He slammed the M-16's butt plate down on the NVA's head so hard one of the guy's eyes popped out of its socket and dangled from the cord of its optic nerve to rest on his blood-soaked cheek.

But a fourth Red, who had closely followed the other three, rose up to a kneeling position and carefully aimed his AK-47 at Popeye's exposed chest. He jerked the trigger in his excitement and the round went high, striking the navy SEAL in the throat.

Popeye felt intense pain and an inability to breath. He coughed and was aware of hot fluid going through his nose as the hole in his neck fluttered during his attempts to draw in air. He grasped at his wound in an involuntary gesture as he stood up. A half-dozen rounds slapped into him almost simultaneously. His body jerked so hard he came off his feet before dropping on the body of the NVA he'd just killed.

The enemy attack formation grew in density as they continued their screaming, insane assault.

"On your feet and move back!" Falconi yelled.

The eight surviving Black Eagles, firing rapidly into the horde of fanatics to their front, continued to drop enemy soldiers as they backed slowly to the rear.

The NVA situated to the back of their battalion were unaware of the true circumstances at the front. Burning with battle lust, the young Reds pressed forward. They stumbled and staggered over the packed carpet of their comrades' corpses as they surged on in an attempt to close with the Black Eagles in front of them. When any of these soldiers finally worked their way to the front, they also dropped in the steady hail of steel Falconi's men threw at them.

But the Black Eagles, despite their accurate fire and large supply of ammunition, were still forced back as overwhelming numbers pressed relentlessly toward them.

Falconi's mind raced. The Black Eagles were like the stupid farm boy who picked up the rattlesnake. They couldn't hang on forever, yet they couldn't let go either.

Once more the detachment commander found himself in the intolerable situation of catching hell from all sides no matter what he did.

Fuck it! Falconi's mind echoed. *Nobody said this job was going to be easy.*

CHAPTER NINETEEN

The taxi pulled up in front of Tsing Chai's mah-jongg parlor. The doorman limped to the vehicle's door and opened it with a polite bow.

Colonel Ngai Quang, unobtrusive in somber civilian attire, noted the bruised condition of the man, but made no comment. He quickly exited the cab and hurried across the short expanse of sidewalk. He entered the establishment, but instead of stopping at any of the gambling tables, hurried toward the rear.

The two guards at the curtained entrance to the hallway leading off the main room barely had room to acknowledge the colonel as he rushed past them and down the dark corridor to Tsing Chai's private office.

He knocked frantically on the door and fidgeted until it was opened to admit him.

Tsing Chai, fat and cherubic, was seated behind his desk. Clad in an expensive silk kimono, he had several ledgers spread out on the desk before him. A husky young guard stood alertly by the entrance to the radio room. Tsing smiled at the colonel. "Ah! *Chao ong, Dại Ta.*"

Ngai's face twitched and he started to speak, but instead he burst out in a fit of nervous coughing.

Tsing motioned to the security man. "Fetch a glass of water quickly. It appears that the joy of *Dại Ta* Ngai's visit is dimmed by his sudden physical distress. Let us hope he is not seriously ill."

The bodyguard went to the wet bar in the corner of the room and returned with a glass of distilled water. He handed it to the colonel without a word, then returned to his post.

Ngai took several sips and cleared his throat. When he was finally able to speak, it was only with a croak. "Are you insane?"

Tsing shrugged. "Not even a cordial greeting from you? Why would you begin a conversation in such an unfriendly manner? And with such an impolite question?"

Ngai fell into another coughing spell and had to take some more water. He breathed heavily. "How could— you have — done something — so stupid?"

Tsing sneered. "Still insisting on addressing him with insulting questions, Ngai?"

Ngai swallowed. Fool! You killed one of Tran's men!"

Tsing frowned. "What are you talking about?"

"His body was found here in the Cholon earlier," Ngai said. "Lying on a trash heap."

"I haven't the slightest idea of what you are speaking about, my dear *Dạ*i Ta Ngai," Tsing said. "The closest thing we had to such a situation was when we were forced to punish a member of my security staff. He was caught prowling in my office. But I assure you—"

"He was a sergeant in the *Canh-sat va cong-an* serving directly under Colonel Tran Hoc!" Ngai exclaimed, his face distorted by fear. "Tran is one of General Nguyen Ngoc Loan's number one men."

Tsing was alarmed enough to raise his enormous bulk off the chair and stand up. "No! This is impossible! My people questioned the thief thoroughly. He divulged no information other than he had attempted to rob me."

"You've made a terrible mistake," Ngai said. "An interdepartment intelligence communication came into my office earlier today. It revealed the death of Sergeant Chin Duc. His body was found in the alley behind the Street of Cho."

Tsing shook his head in a negative manner and forced himself to calm down. He resumed his seat and managed a smile. "Please, my dear *Dai Ta* Ngai," let me assure you that my people have done nothing so stupid." He snapped his fingers at the guard by the door. "Fetch Kahn."

The guard hurried out of the office to tend to the matter.

Ngai wiped at his sweating brow. "This is terrible! Tran must suspect something. Perhaps I am under suspicion from the National Police."

"Calm yourself," Tsing said. "It is unnecessary, and — please forgive me — you are behaving in a manner that is most unflattering to a man of your position."

Within a few moments the door opened and the guard, followed by the gigantic bulk of Tsing's senior security man, entered the office.

Kahn bowed deeply and respectfully to his employer. "Yes, Master Tsing?"

"I have a question to put to you, Kahn," Tsing said

calmly. "I am sure you recall the thief that was apprehended in this office?"

Kahn involuntarily put a meaty hand on his sore ribs. "Yes, Master Tsing."

"Please inform *Da*i Ta Ngai the result of the interrogation you administered to the man caught in my office."

Kahn turned to the colonel. "There was nothing remarkable about it. After we had come upon his act of thievery, we questioned him closely and relentlessly. Even under my best efforts all he would reveal was the fact that he had attempted to rob Master Tsing. It was obvious that the miserable wretch was nothing but a common, ungrateful thief who would rob his employer. After the questioning, we did only what was proper for such a despicable piece of scum."

"And would you be so kind as to inform us of where you disposed of the carrion after he was properly punished?"

"We took the cadaver to the alley behind the Street of Cho."

Ngai shrieked then fell into a faint on the heavy carpet of the office.

The line of green-clad NVA broke through the trees to appear suddenly in the small open space in front of the Black Eagles' defensive perimeter.

"Fire!" Major Robert Falconi ordered in a loud shout.

Eight M-16 rifles spat their 5.56-millimeter slugs out in swarms of steel-jacketed fury that zipped into the compact ranks of the enemy.

The NVA troops took the punishment as their ranks melted in number, the victims tumbling to the ground in bloody clumps. They finally withdrew after enduring five minutes of the roaring hell Falconi and his men threw at them.

Archie Dobbs pressed his hand against the side of his head in an effort to give some relief to his punished eardrums. The roar of firing left him and his buddies nearly deaf.

"I'll say one thing for them fuckers," he said to Lightfingers O'Quinn as he pointed to the pile of Communist dead. "They don't mind dyin'."

"Crazy fuckers," Lightfingers said. "We're all the time running into crazy fuckers."

"Like them Pathet Lao last time, huh?" Archie remarked.

Lightfingers started to reply when he noticed the mass of movement to their direct front. "Shit! Here they come again!"

Battle cries burst out from the vegetation fifty meters away. There was a loud rustling, then another formation of NVA charged into sight from the brush.

Each and every Black Eagle was on full automatic. They covered their individual fields of fire with short bursts, each sweeping back and forth across his particular area of responsibility. It wasn't necessary to aim carefully. The only requirement was to keep the muzzles at the right height and angle to send flights of bullets into the massed target presented to them by the compact formations of Red soldiers.

The detachment's position was a strong one. Slightly elevated, they could look down on their attackers. The right side of their line had the natural cover of an incredibly tangled mass of jungle growth that didn't permit penetration by the NVA. The left flank was anchored to a stretch of swamp and quicksand that denied entry with its own brand of natural blockage. In the right circumstances—with enough men and ammunition—Robert Falconi and his wild crew could have held the line indefinitely.

But they had neither.

Their latest ammo drop had given them plenty, but the need for a massive and rapid expending of rounds was draining their supply. And out of the twelve men who had begun the operation, only eight remained combat effective—a casualty rate of exactly one-third with every possibility it would go higher.

Now, with the North Vietnamese again attacking, the Black Eagles shoved fresh magazines into their weapons and again pumped dozens of rounds into the fanatics who surged toward them in human waves.

And, just as before, their bullets smacked into the attackers knocking them to the ground like bundles of straw dummies. However, each assault, though stopped, moved closer to the defenders than the previous efforts. The ground in front of the detachment was covered with a creeping tide of enemy dead.

The NVA effort broke off again. Calvin Culpepper wiped at the sweat on his ebony forehead. Then he gingerly felt the hot muzzle of his weapon. He cursed and jerked his hand back.

"Burn yourself?" Malpractice asked observing him.

"Nope," Calvin replied. "It just doesn't take me long to feel a rifle barrel."

Malpractice laughed. "That's like the old joke about the horseshoe, right?"

"What old joke?" Calvin asked checking his bandoleers.

"You know," Malpractice said. "Where the guy goes in

he blacksmith's shop and accidentally picks up a hot horseshoe and immediately drops it. The blacksmith laughs at him and asks if he got burnt. The guy says, 'No, it just doesn't take me long to look at a horseshoe.' "

"I don't get it," Calvin said.

"The guy picks up the hot —"

"Fuck it!" Calvin shouted. "Here they come again!"

A wave of NVA riflemen swept out of the cover of the jungle and raced toward their position. Calvin grabbed a grenade from his patrol harness. He pulled the pin and tossed it out toward the enemy soldiers.

The device exploded, flinging shards of shrapnel into the group and bowling them over in to the tall grass. Calvin and Malpractice sprayed the fallen Reds with several fusillades of shots.

Then all was silent again.

Calvin turned to Malpractice. "What was you sayin'?"

"I was explainin' that joke to you," Malpractice answered. "The one about the hot horseshoe."

"It ain't funny," Calvin said.

"Sure it's funny," Malpractice argued. "This dumb sonofabitch picks up a —"

Calvin's eyes narrowed in anger. "Are you callin' me a dumb son-of-a-bitch?"

Malpractice's temper snapped. "I'm explainin' the fuckin' joke to you. Listen, will ya? The dumb son-of-a-bitch I'm talkin' about is the one that touched the hot horseshoe."

"You're callin' me a dumb son-of-a-bitch 'cause I touched my rifle barrel when it was hot, ain't you?"

Malpractice growled and set his M-16 down. He crawled rapidly toward Calvin, hissing under his breath. "I'm gonna kick your wise ass."

"C'mon and try, goddamn it!" Calvin yelled in rage.

Top Gordon, who had been staring unbelievably at the two, rushed forward in a crouch and dove between them. "You're both dumb sons-of-bitches!" he growled. "What the hell do you think you're doing?"

The two stopped and looked at each other. Both were puzzled. Calvin shook his head. "Shit, I don't know."

Malpractice groaned. "Oh, damn! We been out here too long. We almost got into a fist fight over a fuckin' joke."

Top sighed. "My God! We're facing an outfit that out-numbers us twenty or thirty to one — maybe more — and we've gotten so fucked up that we're starting to fight amongst ourselves." He glared at them. "Get back to your positions!"

"Right, Top."

He watched the two withdraw to their posts; then he returned to his own. It seemed that if the enemy didn't break the Black Eagles, the strain of constant combat would.

Falconi, who had been out of sight a few meters away, whispered over to Top Gordon as loudly as he dared. "What the hell was going on over there?"

"You wouldn't believe it, Skipper," Top said. "But when we get out of this shit, you'd better really get these crazy bastards some R&R!"

"Yeah," Falconi agreed. Then he added to himself under his breath. *"If* we get out of this shit."

Pictures of a general's shoulder boards bearing a sin-gle star danced through KGB Colonel Gregori Krash-chenko's head.

He stared out of his office down on the busy streets of Hanoi below the NVA headquarters building, as he sipped the strong tea from the mug he held cupped in both hands.

Colonel Truong Van sat on the window sill next to him. This North Vietnamese intelligence officer had been assigned as the Russian's counterpart in directing operations against the relentless Black Eagle Detachment that had plagued the north over the previous several months. He, like the Soviet colonel, felt a lightness of heart.

"The glorious end of our endeavors is within reach, Comrade Colonel Krashchenko," he said.

"Indeed!" Krashchenko agreed. "Vang and the 327th are virtually sitting on top of Falconi and his men. All he has to do is reach out and grab the imperialist swine."

"I now appreciate your choice of Vang as commander of the operation," Truong admitted. "At first I was not so sure that such an arrangement would work."

"In the KGB we have found the study of human psychology to be of great value," Krashchenko said turning to face the interior of the room. "Even though various nationalities and races each display unique peculiarities, there are certain basic concepts that can be applied to all."

"I must remind you that making a general a battalion commander is tantamount to an insult," Truong said. "It is, in reality, a demotion even if he did keep his rank."

"Yes, of course," Krashchenko said, "but not if you combine such a reduction in leadership responsibility with the assignment of a difficult task."

"A clever move, yes," Truong said.

"You will be even more convinced when Vang delivers

Falconi to us," Krashchenko added.

"He will not do that, Comrade Colonel," Truong said. "He will kill him."

"What do you mean?" the Russian demanded.

"Vang's hatred of this Falconi is based on more than the defeat he suffered on the Song Bo River," Truong said. "There has been an unbearable loss of face involved here."

Krashchenko set the mug down on his desk. "He has been ordered to capture Falconi—and he must do exactly that!"

"Every value and ethic General Vang holds sacred has been violated in this incident. Therefore he has no moral choice but to kill the American," Truong said.

"I will not tolerate such an act!" Krashchenko exclaimed.

The North Vietnamese officer walked to the door and opened it. Before he left the room Truong turned and faced the Soviet officer. "There are certain things about Oriental psychology you have yet to learn, Comrade Colonel Krashchenko!"

CHAPTER TWENTY

A chilling silence enveloped the jungle in front of the Black Eagles' defensive position.

No bird, insect or animal stirred in the pressing heat. Now and then a weak moan would sound from the pile of NVA casualties in the clearing. But for the most part the Red soldiers lay in silent death, forming a thick covering on the rain-forest floor. In some places the cadavers were piled five and six deep.

Master Sergeant Top Gordon, in his job as senior NCO, moved silently from man to man, checking each out. It wasn't much of a task now. He started with Archie Dobbs on the extreme left then worked his way through Malpractice McCorckel, Chun Kim, and Lightfingers O'Quinn before he finally reached the man holding the right flank, Calvin Culpepper. With Sparks Jackson sitting back near Major Robert Falconi, it took the detachment's top soldier only a sparse five minutes to complete his limited rounds.

He crawled back to where Sparks Jackson, his commo gear, and Falconi waited. "We're getting a brief break huh?" the NCO remarked to the commander.

"Yeah," Falconi agreed peering out toward the jungle.

"We don't have much firepower up front, Skipper," Top said. "And we're going to be out of ammo real quick."

Falconi motioned to Sparks. "Drop off your radio with me. You might as well lend a hand on the firing line."

"Aye, aye. sir," the navy commo man said. He looked at Top. "Where do you want me and my trusty shootin' iron?"

"Squirm in between Archie and Malpractice," Top said. "That's about as good a place as any."

"Did you pass out the word to the guys?"

"Right, Skipper. I issued the remaining grenades. Everybody ended up with at least one. I'll fire first on the next attack, and it'll be a signal to toss 'em out. Then the guys will provide their own covering fire and draw back like you said."

"Anybody that gets left behind is going to die," Falconi said.

"I told 'em that too, Skipper. They're ready."

"Well, let's see if our air support is still laid on," Falconi said turning on the radio.

Top watched him recalibrate the instrument. "I sure hope it is, Skipper. It's our only chance."

"That's why I didn't want the rest of the guys to know about it," Falconi explained. "No sense in giving the guys hope if things are fucked up."

"I agree wholeheartedly," Top said. "I remember the times when tired troops on a speed march or tactical movement have asked how much farther they got to go. Some wise-ass officer or noncom would keep telling 'em

216

there was only a hundred meters more. After a coupla hours, they ask again and get the same answer — a hundred meters more."

"No way to run a railroad," Falconi said.

"After a while the troops lose faith and trust," Top said. "It's better to say you don't know or give 'em the bitter truth."

"Or, as in this case, don't tell 'em anything," Falconi added.

"Right!"

The major picked up the transmitter/receiver handset. "Well, we've got no FAC and damned little time. Even if there is aircraft available this might not work."

"I'll keep my fingers crossed," Top said. "If you can —"

He was interrupted by the sudden explosion of sound.

"They're on our asses again, Top," Falconi said.

Out on the front of the line another massed attack rolled toward the Black Eagles. The NVA troops stumbled over the bodies of their previously fallen buddies in a relentless drive to reach their objective.

Archie Dobbs, with the protective swamp on his left, was able to fire on targets of opportunity to his direct front and off to his right. Sparks Jackson's rounds swept slightly into Archie's area of fire, and swung to the left until his bullets began intermingling with Malpractice's. The medic's field of fire swept from that point to combine with Chun Kim's. Both the Korean marine's and Calvin Culpepper's volleys took care of the area on the right flank.

It was this hail of steel that General Vang kept ordering his troops into. Filled with hatred and driven into a frenzy of savage rage by the insane ravings of the battalion's political commissar, the young soldiers of Ho didn't hesitate to rush into the Black Eagles' curtain of fire despite the horrendous casualties they sustained.

Top Gordon had rushed forward to lend a hand. He situated himself to one side of Sparks Jackson not far from Malpractice McCorckel. A thick tree gave him cover as he tried to back up the other two troopers' efforts with his own highly accurate bursts of 5.56-millimeter rounds.

Top gritted his teeth and swore. He knew that each man had two or three more magazines in their final bandoleers.

General Vang took the young company commander's salute. "*Chao ong,* Comrade *Dai Úy,*" the general said. "Are your men ready to be committed to the battle?"

"Yes, Comrade *Thiêú Tu'ó'ng,*" the officer said. "They have grown impatient while being held in reserve during the previous attacks."

Vang smiled. "Good soldiers of socialism! As the battalion's only reinforced company, they have probably been wondering why they've yet to be given the chance to bloody the imperialists."

"I am certain that is so," the captain said. "But their response to the strict training and discipline they've been under has taught them not to question orders."

"Of course," Vang said. "It is because they are so numerous that I've held them back. The capitalist *chó* that we face have now been worn down until they are on their last legs. You and your company now have the honor of administering the final blow to them."

Stahler, sitting nearby, could not understand the exchange between the two. But he could tell from their expressions that the officer had received pertinent combat orders. The East German got to his feet and approached Vang. "I must speak to you, Comrade General."

Vang glared at him. "You wait!" He turned and said a few more words to his subordinate, then dismissed him. He faced Stahler again. "I know what it is you wish to say, and I am telling you now what I've said before — the conversation is closed."

"It is important that we capture Falconi," Stahler argued desperately. "Our comrade Krashchenko wants him. And remember that Falconi is a Russian. The Soviet KGB can get much information from him and use him as a propaganda tool as well.

"I don't give a damn about that," Vang snarled. "And as far as Falconi being a Russian — well, that is all the more reason for him to die!" He took his helmet from a nearby table and slipped it on his head. "Now we are going to make the final charge against the imperialists. And it will be to destroy them!"

"Does your contempt for the Russians extend to us East Germans?" he demanded.

"Perhaps," Vang said coldly.

"Do you realize that I will be held responsible for your actions" Stahler demanded.

"What do I care?" Vang snarled. "Am I to tremble because you disapprove of me? Am I your coolie boy?"

"Of course not," Stahler said.

"Then keep your thoughts to yourself!" Vang admonished him. "And remember *I* am in command here!"

"Then what are our orders, Comrade General? Are we to accompany you on this final spasm of death that will lead to your glorious victory?"

"Your men are exhausted," Vang said. "Our native

mountains and jungles are too much for them. Leave them where they are — sprawled out in the jungle behind these bunkers." He walked to the exit of the dugout.

Stahler, so angry he trembled, watched Vang leave.

Falconi gripped the radio's handset with such force his knuckles were white. He spoke into it again. "Fireball, this is Black Eagle. Over."

The combat in front had grown in intensity. A marked increase in firing had evolved on both sides of the battle line.

Falconi had been attempting to establish commo for the previous half hour. Now he spoke desperately, angrily. "Goddamn it! Fireball, this is Black Eagle! Over!"

Suddenly a voice crackled in his ear. "Well, goddamn it yourself, Black Eagle. This is Fireball. What can I do for you? Over."

Falconi grinned at the sound of the pilot's voice coming in over the radio. "Glad to see they kept you laid on for this mission. I got a target for you, Fireball. But it's right in our laps. I hope you're good. Over."

"Black Eagle," the pilot enjoined. "I'm navy — that means I'm *damned* good! Let's get on with this mission. Over."

"Roger," Falconi said. "Grid coordinates for the strike are one-eight-five-two-five-one-zero-six-seven-five. Over." He waited while the pilot repeated the numbers. "There's a small clearing there. Hit the north side. We're on the south. Over."

"Roger. Got a target description for me? Over?"

"That's it, baby," Falconi said. "I hope you're damned good like you say. Over."

"Hell, I ain't damned good, son, I'm *god*damned

220

good. Now you hang on. Here we come!"

Falconi gritted his teeth. That navy pilot had better be among the best. Only a few scant meters separated the fighting forces. Any miscalculation by the aircraft commander would result in the Black Eagles being destroyed along with the NVA.

Oh, well! Falconi sighed to himself. *Nobody said this fucking job was going to be easy!*

General Vang stood in front of the Third Company of the 327th Infantry Battalion of the North Vietnamese Army. He pulled his Russian Tokarev pistol from its holster and waved it in the air.

"A few months ago many of your comrades were slaughtered in a battle with the imperialist swine!" he yelled. "Now the same Running Dogs of Wall Street are only fifty meters ahead of us in this jungle. For the previous two days other companies of this glorious battalion have hurled themselves at the enemy until the swine are worn down. It is time for the final blow that will wipe the scum from the face of the earth in this struggle to expand socialism to our brothers in the south. Every soldier must do his duty!"

Loud cheers erupted from the assembled troops.

Vang pointed to the front with his pistol. "Men of the Third Company!" he screamed. "Advance!"

The young Communists, burning with a deep desire to destroy their enemy, surged forward after the general.

Sparks Jackson pulled the charging handle back on the M-16 and let it slide home. A jammed round had caused a delay in his firing at the massed enemy ahead of him. The solid clack of the weapon's mechanism told him a fresh round was now seated. The navy SEAL put the rifle to his shoulder and raised it to fire.

The Russian 7.62-millimeter bullet smacked into his forehead.

Sparks didn't jump from the force of the slug's entry. His face dropped to the jungle dirt and he lay still. No limb jerked and he made no sound.

Ten meters behind him, Falconi strained his ears. When he finally heard the sounds of the Navy Corsair prop-driven, ground-support aircraft, he screamed as loud as he could. "Hit the dirt! Hit the dirt!"

The Black Eagles, though individualistic to the nth degree, had enough exposure to their commander to obey him instantly — almost instinctively — when he issued an order. Every man went down even lower than his prone position and stuck his face into the stinking jungle soil.

The roar of aircraft engines was sudden and unexpected. Hot shell casings cascaded down on Falconi and his men as the trees and vegetation in front of them vibrated with the .50-caliber slugs that slammed into them. The living beings there — the unfortunate NVAs — were swept to the ground by the force of the aerial attack.

Vang, with the Third Company massed behind him, ran through the trees waving the Russian pistol.

The roar of the fighting grew louder as he neared the front lines and he found the sound exhilarating. He reached the first corpses of previous attacks. The bodies of a few soldiers were sprawled out grotesquely among the bushes. But the bodies increased in number until the general found it difficult to negotiate them. Although he almost tripped and fell several times, he continued to press forward, looking back to see if the young soldiers behind him were still following.

They were.

At this point Vang and his men were climbing up and down small mounds of their dead comrades. The sound of weaponry grew so loud that it was deafening. Then, surprisingly, it died off slightly.

Vang, negotiating his way through the cadavers, finally reached his front lines. He started to yell encouragement to the men there, but when he raised his eyes, his mouth fell open in pure astonishment.

For a brief, blinding second he caught sight of three aircraft, close together, appearing only a few meters above treetop level. The NVA general could tell by the rapid flashing on their wings that they were firing.

Immediately there was a whipping around him and a nearby soldier's torso seemed to explode in a red splash of blood and intestines while another's head simply vanished.

Vang managed to take a couple of startled steps backward before three of the large machine-gun rounds smashed into his chest and hurled him, somersaulting, back into the disintegrating ranks of the glorious Third Company.

CHAPTER TWENTY-ONE

The Corsairs roared in for the sixth time, then pulled up and zoomed out of sight, the sounds of their engines quickly dying off.

"Black Eagle, this is Fireball. Over."

Falconi, his punished ears barely able to hear, hit the transmission button on the handset. "Fireball, this is Black Eagle. Way to go. You're not only good, *god*-damned good—you guys are the *god*damned best. Over."

"We thank you Black Eagle. Need any more passes? Over."

"Negative, Fireball. We'll take it from here. I'm hereby awarding you three Way-to-Gos and a great big Atta-Boy. Much thanks. Over."

"Roger, Black Eagle. Out."

Falconi rose from his sitting position and grasped the radio. He trotted forward to where Sparks Jackson was located, between Archie and Malpractice. He spotted the navy man lying in his position.

"Hey, Sparks," Falconi said. "This fucking radio's too

heavy for me. I'm giving it—"

Then he sensed something strange in the way Sparks lay, so still. Archie Dobbs got up from his own fighting area and walked up to Sparks and knelt down. He rolled him over. "Shit."

"Another good man gone," Falconi said.

"Who was it?" Top Gordon asked walking up.

"Sparks," Falconi said. He slung the radio on his back. "I'll handle the commo chores myself from here on out. Let's get the guys formed up and move forward. There're still those East Germans to deal with."

The surviving six Black Eagles fell into a skirmish line in front of their commander and advanced from their former defensive positions into the clearing.

The small area was wall-to-wall bodies. There was not one square inch of open space. The only way they could negotiate their way across was to walk on top of the dead. Now and then a badly wounded NVA, deep in shock, would stare, unconceiving, up at them as they passed over him.

The going got rougher when they reached the opposite side of the little blood-splattered glade. Here the cadavers were not only piled on top of each other, but were lying on crushed bushes. Some, sprawled face-up, seemed to give the Black Eagles accusing glares in their expressions of death. In some instances they had to shove the corpses aside in order to have the room to continue on their way.

But eventually the number and density of enemy dead thinned out and the going got better. Archie Dobbs, walking ahead of their sparse line, suddenly signaled a halt. He deftly moved back a few steps, then turned and hurried back to Falconi.

"Bunkers up ahead, Skipper," the scout said.

"Any troops around them?"

"Only our Kraut buddies," Archie reported. "They're armed and are wearing all their gear."

"Let's have a look."

Falconi and Archie, with the rest of the detachment squatting down to wait, moved up to a vantage point in order to take a look into the area.

Although on alert, the East German soldiers were obviously in a bad physical state. A couple, their heads bobbing, fought drifting off to sleep while their comrades stood around in lethargic attitudes, just barely hanging on to their American rifles.

Archie grinned. "Them guys is tuckered fuckers."

"They'll come alive quick enough if they have to," Falconi cautioned him.

"I'd guess they don't know what the hell happened up there in the fight," Archie surmised. "They're prob'ly waiting for the NVA assholes to come back and take 'em off to the north."

"Yeah," Falconi said. "Let's get back to the others."

Using stealth and care, the pair pulled away, then turned and hurried back to where Top Gordon and the four other Black Eagles were waiting.

The detachment commander wasted no time in calling them together. "The East Germans are gathered around a bunch of bunkers back there," Falconi explained. "They're pooped out, but have plenty of fight left in 'em, no doubt. I want Kim and Lightfingers to move into a position about twenty-five meters on the other side of their position."

"Right, Skipper," Lightfingers said

"If — or I should say *when* — they come your way, you'll

have to stop 'em," Falconi went on. "It'll be up to you to convince the bastards that there's a dozen or so of you out there."

"Shit!" Kim swore. "Too bad all M-79 rounds gone."

"Do your best with full auto on those M-16s," Falconi said. "The rest of us will hit 'em up front."

"We'll need about a half hour to get into position, Skipper," Lightfingers said.

"Go!"

Without another word the two marines, one American and the other South Korean, moved out on their mission.

The remained of the detachment settled down and waited as Falconi checked his watch. They weren't in much better shape than the adversaries they were about to face. Though better conditioned and acclimated than the East Germans, the Black Eagles had been in constant combat for many hours. The toll of the previous fighting, combined with the fact this was their third mission without a break, had left them with blank-eyed stares and slow, lethargic movements.

When the half hour was up, Falconi got to his feet. "Let's go guys. As skirmishers right along here."

He watched as Top Gordon, Archie Dobbs, Malpractice McCorckel, and Calvin Culpepper formed up in front of him as a single line of riflemen.

Falconi also wondered which of them would die in this final spasm of Operation Asian Blitzkrieg.

"I don't like it," Kamerad Leutnant Willi Feldhaus complained to his commander.

Stahler, his eyes red-rimmed, looked at his second-in-command and sighed. "There's nothing to be done about it, Willi. If Vang made up his mind to wipe out the *Schwarzenadler* to the last man, there's no way we can stop him."

"But will we be held responsible, *Kamerad Hauptmann*?"

Stahler shrugged. "I don't know." They were sitting outside Vang's bunker. All the NVA had gone to the final attack while the East Germans remained behind. The sounds of the fighting had been continuous and confusing. Some of the Europeans thought they had even heard aircraft. The captain started to say something else when a voice interrupted him from the jungle.

"Achtung!"

Feldhaus spun and faced the sound of the call. "Now who in *Hölle* is that?"

The voice hollered out again. "You Krautheads throw down your weapons and give it up, *verstehen Sie?*"

Feldhaus gasped, "It's the *Schwarzenadler!*"

Stahler didn't waste a second. *"Zuruckziehen zu der Dschungel!"* he ordered his men.

They responded immediately by running toward the tree line behind the bunkers. They progressed only a few meters into the wild country before a fusillade of shots ripped into them.

Lightfingers and Kim, laying in ambush, did their job with deadly efficiency.

Willie Feldhaus continued forward until he was stitched across the chest by three shots. He dropped his weapon and clutched at his mangled body, the blood flowing out in crimson sheets. The German staggered a few steps to pitch forward soundlessly. He crashed through the palm frond that served Lightfingers O'Quinn as cover.

Confused and panic-stricken, the other East Europeans pulled away from the roaring hell and made an effort to return to the bunkers. They found themselves in a crossfire which dropped the remainder of their group in writhing, bloody bundles of humanity.

Rolf Stahler, leading them back, was missed in the initial volleys and managed to dive into Vang's bunker. He wasted no time in taking up a position at a firing slit and shooting back at the Black Eagles.

There was an exchange of shots that went on for several minutes. Falconi finally ordered his men to stop firing. He crawled as far forward as he dared, and yelled at the bunker.

"Hey, Kraut! You understand English."

There was no anser.

"I am the commanding officer of this detachment. I know your nationality, Kraut," Falconi said. "I promise you that you'll not be killed if you surrender to us."

An explosion of shots erupted from the bunker.

Archie Dobbs, not far away, rushed from a nearby supply dugout he'd been exploring. He threw himself down beside Falconi. The scout showed his commander an object he had. "Looky here, Skipper. It's a Russian grenade. I know enough of their alphabet to have read the stenciling on the box it was in. The words was *konkusyanya granáta*—sounds like concussion grenade to me."

"That's an accurate translation," Falconi said. "Where did you learn to read Russian?" Falconi asked.

"I can't speak it like you. I only learned their alphabet, Skipper," Archie explained. "At the end of my first hitch, when I was in the 82nd Airborne, I decided to make something of myself. So rather than reenlist for my own vacancy when my ETS came up, I decided to get some sort of an education. The reenlistment NCO said there was several openings in the Russian course at the Army Language School in Monterrey. It sounded good to me, so I signed up. They gave me a preliminary course at Fort Bragg before I reported in." He grinned sheepishly. "But I got involved in a misunderstanding over my platoon sergeant's girl in town. There was a sort of ruckus over the incident."

"And you ended up in the stockade," Falconi said to complete the story. "But at least you managed to learn enough to make out the words. And you want to use that concussion grenade?"

"You bet, Skipper!"

"Let's give it a try then," Falconi said. "We'll cover you."

"Right, Skipper."

Archie waited until the detachment set up a rapid covering fire, then he rushed forward to a point within range. He pulled the pin and threw a side-armed toss at the firing slit. The grenade bounced once — twice — then straight into the bunker.

Clouds of dust rolled out with the explosion.

Archie leaped to his feet and rushed inside as the rest of the Black Eagles charged forward. By the time they arrived at the dugout entrance, the scout had reappeared dragging an unconscious figure with him.

Falconi bent down and examined the man.

In a few moments the stunned soldier opened his eyes. They fluttered as he focused them on the man in front of him. Stahler blinked and frowned. *"Ist du der Major Falconi?"*

Falconi's knowledge of German was only the rudimentary brand he had picked up while stationed in

Europe. But he knew enough to form one crude sentence:

"*Ja,*" he answered. "*Und du ist ein* shithead."

EPILOGUE

The C-130 eased over onto the proper heading and slowly lost altitude. The pilot continued his gradual descent, finally easing back as the big aircraft's tires squealed in protest on contact with the concrete runway of Tan Son Nhut Air Base.

The plane taxied down the runway, but instead of turning to the general disembarking area, it steered into the opposite direction. It's destination was an area without a hangar where a small building surrounded by barbed wire stood.

Chuck Fagin and Andrea Thuy stood in front of the gate leading to the compound. The C-130 came to a stop in front of them. The two watched as a side door opened and the crew chief dropped the step-ladder to facilitate the passengers' exit.

The first man off was Major Robert Falconi. Clad in battle gear and incredibly soiled and sweat-soaked camouflaged fatigues, his exhaustion was evident even from a distance. He turned to watch his first two men off. Archie Dobbs and Malpractice McCorckel had a stretcher between them. A body covered by a poncho rested on it.

After they had stepped down to the runway, Calvin Culpepper and Chun Kim followed. They, too, bore a litter, and this one's burden was also a corpse.

A stranger, his hands bound behind his back, came off after them while Top Gordon, with one hand tightly grasping the prisoner, pushed him along.

Fagin stepped forward as they walked up. He pointed to the dead men. "Who are they?" he asked.

"Sparks Jackson and Dinky Dow," Falconi answered. "They were the only bodies we could recover. Tommy Newcomb, Horny Galchaser, and Popeye Jenkins are still out there. I've noted the locations of their graves — except for Horny — so they can be recovered and sent home."

"I take it Galchaser's body was policed up by the enemy," Fagin said.

"Right."

"I'm sorry, Falcon," Fagin said. "About him — and the others."

"Yeah. Well, they got a little sloppy," Falconi said coldly. "Men have a tendency to do that. Especially if they're pushed to the limit — or beyond."

Andrea Thuy took Falconi's arm, her eyes soft and caring. "Wait, Robert. Don't say anything yet. There are things you must find out."

Falconi's jaw tightened. "There are already *things* that I've found out."

Fagin's expression remained calm. "This is the prisoner, of course," he said as Top Gordon shoved the man forward.

"Yeah," Falconi said. "His name is Rolf Stahler, a captain in the East German police."

"I have some MPs to turn him over to," Fagin said. "They'll take care of him."

"Think we can make a good case in the UN from this bastard?" Falconi asked. "He's walking-talking proof that American troops didn't commit those war crimes up in the northern operational areas."

"It doesn't matter," Fagin said. "He won't be used for that anyhow. A quick exchange has been arranged for one of our people captured in Czechoslovakia."

"What?" Falconi asked angrily. "The only reason for our mission was to prove to the world that Reds were committing atrocities while disguised as U.S. troops."

"They'll never know now," Fagin said. "I guess the upper echelon figures the change of prisoners was more important."

"Shit!"

Fagin watched the rest of the detachment go inside the building. "I know how you feel."

"No you don't!" Falconi snapped. "And I'm going to tell you something here and now, Fagin! My boys are going on R&R, understand? This was their third time out into the war without a break."

"They'll be staying here in Saigon," Fagin said.

"Good."

"But not on R&R," he added.

"What the hell are you talking about?"

I'm not going to give it to you easy, Falconi," Fagin said "I'm about to let you have it right between the eyes."

"I wish to hell you would," Falconi remarked.

"The Reds not only knew every move you made out there, but when and how you were going to do it?"

"What the fuck are you talking about, Fagin?" Falconi demanded. "Who told 'em?"

"I did."

"You did!"

Fagin walked toward the gate leading to the interior of the compound. "Come on. Like Andrea said—there's a hell of a lot you've got to find out."

"Damn, Fagin. You can start cluing me in anytime."

"Let me begin with this cheerful bit of news," Fagin said. "At this very moment you and the Black Eagles are heading for a showdown in Saigon."

McLEANE'S RANGERS
by John Darby

#1: BOUGAINVILLE BREAKOUT   (1207, $2.50)

Even the Marines call on McLeane's Rangers, the toughest, meanest, and best fighting unit in the Pacific. Their first adventure pits the Rangers against the entire Japanese garrison in Bougainville. The target—an ammo depot invulnerable to American air attack . . . and the release of a spy.

#2: TARGET RABAUL   (1271, $2.50)

Rabaul—it was one of the keys to the control of the Pacific and the Japanese had a lock on it. When nothing else worked, the Allies called on their most formidable weapon—McLeane's Rangers, the fearless jungle fighters who didn't know the meaning of the word quit!

#3: HELL ON HILL 457   (1343, $2.50)

McLeane and his men make a daring parachute drop in the middle of a heavily fortified Jap position. And the Japs are dug in so deep in a mountain pass fortress that McLeane may have to blow the entire pass to rubble—and his men in the bargain!

Available wherever paperbacks are sold, or order direct from the Publisher. Send cover price plus 50¢ per copy for mailing and handling to Zebra Books, 475 Park Avenue South, New York, N.Y. 10016. DO NOT SEND CASH.